'We're all still here, Ginny, waiting for you to emerge and be our friend again.'

'I can't.'

'No,' he said, and because he couldn't stop himself he touched her cheek, a feather touch, because the need to touch her was irresistible and she was so beautiful and fearful and needful.

So Ginny.

'You can't,' he said. 'But tonight you did.'

And then, before he knew what he was going to do, before she could possibly know for he hadn't even realised he was about to do it himself, he stooped and he kissed her lightly on the lips.

It was another feather touch. He'd backed away before she even realised he'd done it, appalled with himself, putting space between them, moving away before she could react with the fear he knew was in her.

But he had to say it.

'We're all here waiting,' he said into the dark. 'We'll wait for as long as it takes. This island is as old as time itself and it has all the patience in the world.'

And as if on cue the world trembled.

Dear Reader

New Zealand is known as 'the shaky isles' for good reason. Last year an earthquake ripped apart the New Zealand city of Christchurch, leaving the city we've all grown to love in ruins.

My friend, fellow author Alison Roberts, was in the centre of it, back working as a paramedic, doing all she could for the city she calls home.

Afterwards we talked about the emotions such an appalling event engenders, how tragedy can so often bring out the best in us. Of course then, as romance writers, our thoughts went to *What if?*

An earthquake such as Christchurch's was simply too big, too dreadful for us to contemplate writing about, but what if we took the same event in a closed community—a tiny island where the islanders need to work together, where past emotions are put aside for present need, where men and women are placed in deadly peril and by that peril discover the things that are most important to them?

In life, love can be hidden, pain can be concealed, but when the earth shakes everything is raw and exposed. Humour, courage, love…they're the cornerstones of our lives, but often it takes tragedy to reveal it. We hope you love reading our *Earthquake!* duet as our heroes and heroines find happiness amid a world that's shaken and is now resettling on a different axis.

Marion Lennox

ALWAYS THE HERO by Alison Roberts
is also available this month
from Mills & Boon® Medical Romance™

MIRACLE ON KAIMOTU ISLAND

BY
MARION LENNOX

First published in Great Britain 2013
by Mills & Boon, an imprint of Harlequin (UK) Limited.
Harlequin (UK) Limited, Eton House, 18-24 Paradise Road,
Richmond, Surrey TW9 1SR

© Marion Lennox 2013

ISBN: 978 0 263 23371 1

enewable
:ustainable
to the

Marion Lennox is a country girl, born on an Australian dairy farm. She moved on—mostly because the cows just weren't interested in her stories! Married to a 'very special doctor', Marion writes Medical Romances™, as well as Mills & Boon® Romances. (She used a different name for each category for a while—if you're looking for her past Romances search for author Trisha David as well.) She's now had well over 90 novels accepted for publication.

In her non-writing life Marion cares for kids, cats, dogs, chooks and goldfish. She travels, she fights her rampant garden (she's losing) and her house dust (she's lost). Having spun in circles for the first part of her life, she's now stepped back from her 'other' career, which was teaching statistics at her local university. Finally she's reprioritised her life, figured out what's important, and discovered the joys of deep baths, romance and chocolate. Preferably all at the same time!

Recent titles by the same author:

In Mills & Boon® Medical Romance™

In Mills & Boon® Romance

These books are also available in eBook format from www.millsandboon.co.uk

To the men and women of Christchurch—
and to one amazing paramedic.
Rosie, you're awesome.

PROLOGUE

NO ONE KNEW how old Squid Davies was. The locals of Kaimotu could hardly remember the time he'd given up his fishing licence, much less when he'd been a lad.

Now his constant place was perched on the oil drums behind the wharf, where the wind couldn't douse a man's pipe, where the sun hit his sea-leathered face and where he could see every boat that went in and out of Kaimotu harbour. From here he could tell anyone who listened what he knew—and he did know.

'She'll be a grand day at sea today, boys,' he'd say, and the locals would set their sights on the furthest fishing grounds, or 'She'll be blowing a gale by midnight,' and who needed the official forecasters? Kaimotu's fishermen knew better than to argue. They brought their boats in by dusk.

But now...

'She's going to be bigger'n that one that hit when my dad's dad was a boy,' Squid intoned in a voice of doom. 'I know what my grandpa said, and it's here now. Pohutukawa trees are flowering for the second time. Mutton birds won't leave their chicks. They should be long gone by now, leaving the chicks to follow, but they won't leave 'em. And then there's waves hitting the shore on Beck's Beach. They don't come in from the north in April—it's not natural. I tell you, the earth moved in 1886 and this'll be bigger.'

It had to be nonsense, the locals told themselves nervously. There'd been one earth tremor two weeks back, enough to crack a bit of plaster, break some crockery, but the seismologists on the mainland, with all the finest technology at their disposal, said a tremor was all there was to it. If ever there was a sizeable earthquake it'd be on the mainland, on the fault line, through New Zealand's South Island, not here, on an island two hundred miles from New Zealand's northern most tip.

But: 'There's rings round the moon, and even the oyster-catchers are keeping inland,' Squid intoned, and the locals tried to laugh it off but didn't quite manage it. The few remaining summer tourists made weak excuses to depart, and the island's new doctor, who was into omens in a big way, decided she didn't want to live on Kaimotu after all.

'Will you cut it out?' Ben McMahon, Kaimotu's only remaining doctor, squared off with Squid in exasperation. 'You've lost us a decent doctor. You're spooking the tourists and locals alike. Go back to weather forecasting.'

'I'm only saying what I'm feelin',' Squid said morosely, staring ominously out at the horizon. 'The big 'un's coming. Nothing surer.'

CHAPTER ONE

PREDICTIONS OF EARTHQUAKES. Hysteria. One lone doctor. Dr Ben McMahon was busy at the best of times and now there weren't enough hours in the day to see everyone who wanted to be seen. His clinic was chaos.

There was, though, another doctor on the island, even though she'd declared she was no longer practising medicine. Up until now Ben had let Ginny be, but Squid's doomsday forecasting meant he needed her.

Again?

The last time Ben McMahon had asked anything of Guinevere Koestrel he'd been down on one knee, as serious as a seventeen-year-old boy could be, pouring his teenage heart out to the woman he adored.

And why wouldn't he adore her? She'd been his friend since she was eight, ever since Ginny's parents had bought the beautiful island vineyard as their hobby/holiday farm and Ben's mother had become Ginny's part-time nanny. They'd wandered the island together, fished, swum, surfed, fought, defended each other to the death—been best friends.

But that last summer hormones had suddenly popped up everywhere. On the night of his ill-advised proposal Ginny had been wearing a fabulous gown, bought by her wealthy parents for the island's annual New Year's Eve Ball. He'd been wearing an ill-fitting suit borrowed from a neighbour. Her appearance had stunned him.

But social differences were dumb, he'd told himself. Suddenly it had seemed vital to his seventeen-year-old self that they stay together for ever.

Surely she could change her plans to study medicine in Sydney, he told her. He planned to be a doctor, too. There was a great medical course in Auckland and he'd won a scholarship. If he worked nights he could manage it, and surely Ginny could join him.

But the seventeen-year-old Ginny had smiled—quite kindly—and told him he was nuts. Her life was in Sydney. The tiny New Zealand island of Kaimotu was simply a place where she and her parents came to play. Besides, she had no intention of marrying a man who called her Carrots.

That had been twelve years ago. Ben had long since put the humiliation of adolescent love behind him, but now there was a more important question. Ginny had been back on the island for six months now. She'd signalled in no uncertain terms that she wanted privacy but Ginny Koestrel was a doctor and a doctor was what the island needed. Now. Which was why, even though looking at her brought back all sorts of emotions he'd thought he'd long suppressed, he was asking yet again.

'Ginny, I need you.'

But the answer would be the same—he knew it. Ginny was surrounded by grapevines, armed with a spray gun, and she was looking at him like he was an irritating interruption to her work.

'I'm sorry, Ben, but I have no intention of working as a doctor again. I have no intention of coming near your clinic. Meanwhile, if these vines aren't sprayed I risk black rot. If you don't mind...'

She squirted her spray gun at the nearest vine. She wasn't

good. She sprayed too high and lost half the mist to the breeze.

Ben lifted the spray pack from her back, aimed the gun at the base of the vine and watched the spray drift up through the foliage.

'Vaccination is one of my many medical skills,' he told her, settling a little, telling himself weird emotions were simply a reaction to shared history, nothing to do with now. They both watched as the spray settled where it should, as emotions settled where they should. 'There's a good vine, that didn't hurt at all, did it?' he said, adopting his very best professional tone. 'If you grow good grapes next year, the nice doctor will give you some yummy compost.' He grinned at the astounded Ginny. 'That's the way you should treat 'em, Carrots. Didn't they teach you anything in your fancy medical school?'

Ginny flushed. 'Cut it out, Ben, and don't you dare call me Carrots. In case you haven't noticed, it's auburn.' She hauled her flaming curls tighter into the elastic band, and glowered.

'Ginny, then.'

'And not Ginny either. And I'm a farmer, not a doctor.'

'I don't actually care who you are,' Ben said, deciding he needed to be serious if he was to have a chance of persuading her. 'You have a medical degree, and I'm desperate. It's taken me twelve months to find a family doctor to fill old Dr Reg's place. Dr Catherine Bolt seemed eminently sensible, but she's lived up to her name. One minor earth tremor and she's bolted back to the mainland.'

'You're kidding.'

'I'm not kidding.' He raked his hand through his hair, remembering how relieved he'd been when the middle-aged Catherine had arrived and how appalled he'd felt when she'd left. He really was alone.

'Every New Zealander has felt earth tremors,' he told Ginny. 'We're not known as the shaky isles for nothing. But you know Squid's set himself up as Forecaster of Doom. With no scientific evidence at all he's been droning on about double flowers of the pohutukawa tree and strange tides and weird bird behaviour and every portent of catastrophe he can think of. There's something about a shrivelled fisherman with a blackened pipe and a voice of doom that gets the natives twitchy. 'As well as losing us our doctor, I now have half the islanders demanding a year's supply of medication so they can see out the apocalypse.'

She smiled, but faintly. 'So you want me on hand for the end of the world?'

'There's no scientific evidence that we're heading for a major earthquake,' he said with dangerous calm. 'But we do have hysteria. Ginny, help me, please.'

'I'm sorry, Ben, but no.'

'Why on earth did you do medicine if you won't practise?'

'That's my business.'

He stared at her in baffled silence. She was a different woman from the one he'd proposed to twelve years ago, he thought. Well, of course she would be. His mother had outlined a sketchy history she'd winkled out of the returning Ginny, a marriage ending in tragedy, but...but...

For some reason he found himself looking at the elastic band. Elastic band? A Koestrel?

Ginny's parents were the epitome of power and wealth. Her father was a prominent Sydney neurosurgeon and her mother's sole purpose was to play society matron. Twice a year they spent a month on the island, in the vineyard they'd bought—no doubt as a tax deduction—flying in their friends, having fabulous parties.

The last time he'd seen Ginny she'd been slim, beautiful, but also vibrant with life. She'd been bouncy, glowing, aching to start medicine, aching to start life. Ready to thump him if he still called her Carrots.

In the years since that youthful proposal he'd realised how wise she'd been not to hurl herself into marriage at seventeen. He'd forgiven her—nobly, he decided—and he'd moved on, but in the back of his mind she'd stayed bouncy, vibrant and glowing. Her mother had carefully maintained her fabulous exterior and he'd expected Ginny to do the same.

She hadn't. The Ginny he was facing now wore elastic bands. Worse, she looked…grim. Flat.

Old? She couldn't be thirty, and yet… How much had the death of a loved one taken out of her?

Did such a death destroy life?

'Ginny—'

'No,' she snapped. 'I've come back to work the vineyard, and that's all.'

'The harvest is long over.'

'I don't care. I'm spraying for…something, whatever Henry told me I had to spray for. When I finish spraying I need to gear up for pruning. Henry's decided to retire and I need to learn. I'm sorry, Ben, but I'm no longer a doctor. I'm a winemaker. Good luck with finding someone who can help you.'

And then she paused. A car was turning into the driveway. A rental car.

It must be Sydney friends, Ben thought, come over on the ferry, but Ginny wasn't dressed for receiving guests. She was wearing jeans, an ancient windcheater, no make-up and she had mud smeared on her nose. A Koestler welcoming guests looking like a farmhand? No and no and no.

'Now what?' she said tightly, and she took the spray pack from Ben and turned to another vine. 'Have you brought re-inforcements? Don't you know I have work to do?'

'This isn't anyone to do with me,' Ben said, and watched

who was climbing out of Kaimotu's most prestigious hire car. The guy looked like a businessman, he thought, and a successful one at that. He was sleek, fortyish, wearing an expensive suit and an expression of disdain as he glanced around at the slightly neglected vineyard. The man opened the trunk and tossed out a holdall. Then he opened the back car door—and tugged out a child.

She was a little girl, four or five years old. She almost fell as her feet hit the ground, but the man righted her as if she was a thing, not a person.

'Guinevere Koestrel?' he called, and headed towards them, tugging the child beside him. 'I'm Richard Harris, from Harris, Styne and Wilkes, partners in law from Sydney. You were expecting me? Or you were expecting the child?'

There was a long silence while Ginny simply stared, dumbstruck, at the incongruous couple approaching.

'I...I guess,' she managed at last. 'But not yet.'

The lawyer was tugging the child closer and as he did...

Down's syndrome, Ben thought. The markers were obvious. The little girl was beautifully dressed, her neat black hair was cropped into a smart little cut, there was a cute hair ribbon perched on top—but nothing could distract from the Down's features.

He glanced back at Ginny, and he saw every vestige of colour had drained from her face. Instinctively he put out a hand to steady her and she grabbed it, as desperately as if she'd been drowning.

'I didn't expect...' she said. 'I thought...this wouldn't happen for months. The legal processes...'

'Our client was prepared to pay whatever was needed to free her to go to Europe,' the man said, clipped and formal. 'We sent you emails. We received no response and we had no phone contact. Our client left the country last Friday, giving us no choice but to bring her. We had a nanny accompany us to New Zealand but the girl gets seasick and refused to come on the ferry.'

He gazed down at the child, and at the look on his face Ben wondered how much leverage had been applied to make such a man do a job like this. A lot, he was sure.

'I don't…I don't check emails any more,' Ginny managed, and the lawyer looked at her as if she was a sandwich short of a picnic. A woman who didn't check emails? His expression said she must be as disabled as the child beside him.

But… 'No matter,' he said, making a hasty recovery. 'My only fear was that I wouldn't find you, but now you're here this is the official handover. According to the documents we mailed to you last month, you've accepted responsibility for her. Her mother's left for Europe. Her instructions were to deliver her to you and here she is.'

And he propelled her forward, pushing her away from him, a little girl in a pretty pink dress, with pink sandals and an expression that said she didn't have one idea of what was happening to her.

If she weren't a Down's child, she'd be sobbing, Ben thought, but he knew enough about the syndrome to know sobbing was a last resort. But still…

'Oh, my…' Ginny said faintly, and Ben's hold on her tightened still further. He'd seen patients in shock before, and Ginny was showing every symptom.

'Ginny, what is this? What's going on?'

Ginny gave herself a shake, as if trying to rid herself of a nightmare. She, too, was staring down at the child. 'I… This is…'

She stopped and looked helplessly towards the lawyer and then at the little girl beside him. 'Tell him,' she said weakly. 'Please…tell Ben.'

And the lawyer was happy to comply. He was obviously

wanting a businesslike response and it looked like he'd decided Ben was the most likely to give it.

'This is Barbara Carmody,' the man said, clipped and efficient, not even looking at the little girl as he introduced her. 'The child's the result of an extra-marital affair between my client and Dr Koestrel's late husband. Her mother raised her with her other two children but unfortunately her husband has finally discovered that the child isn't his. He's rejected her. The marriage has failed and Mrs Carmody has left for Europe.'

'Her parents have deserted her?' Ben said incredulously.

'There are provisions for her care,' the lawyer said smoothly. 'Dr Koestrel's late husband left funds in his will for this eventuality, and there are institutions that will take her. On Mrs Carmody's instructions we contacted Dr Koestrel for the release of those funds but instead of releasing money she's agreed to take on her care. So here she is. The paperwork's all in her suitcase. If you need to contact her mother, do it through us—the address is with her papers. If you could sign the included documents and forward them to our office I'd appreciate it. If you'll excuse me, I don't wish to miss the return ferry. Good afternoon.'

And he turned back towards the car.

The little girl didn't move. Neither did Ginny.

The man was about to walk away and leave the child behind.

No.

Ben strode to the car, slammed closed the car door the lawyer was attempting to open then set himself between lawyer and car while Ginny stood in stunned, white-faced silence.

The little girl didn't move. She didn't look at the lawyer. She didn't look at anyone.

'Abandoning a child's a criminal offence,' Ben said, quite

mildly, looking from the little girl to Ginny and back again. Ginny was staring at the child as if she was seeing a ghost. 'There must be formal proceedings...'

'I'll miss my ferry,' the man said. 'Dr Koestrel has signed the most important documents. Additional paperwork can be sent later.'

'You can't dump a child because you'll miss your ferry,' Ben said, and folded his arms, settling back, not understanding what was going on but prepared to be belligerent until he did.

'Dr Koestrel's agreed to take her. I'm not dumping anyone.'

'So...what did you say? Barbara's the result of an affair between some woman and...Ginny's late husband? Ginny, can you explain?'

'W-wait,' Ginny managed. She looked helplessly at the little girl and then something seemed to firm. Shock receded a little, just a little. She took a deep breath and reached out and took the little girl's hand.

She led her to the edge of the vines, where a veggie garden was loaded with the remains of a rich autumn harvest. Lying beside the garden was a hose. She turned it on and a stream of water shot out.

'Barbara,' she said, crouching with water squirting out of the hose. 'Can you give my tomatoes a drink while we talk? Can you do that for us?

The little girl looked at the hose, at the enticing stream of water. She gave the merest hint of a smile. Whatever had been happening in this child's life in the last few days, Ben thought, she needed time out and somehow Ginny had a sense of how to give it to her.

'Yes,' the girl said, and Ginny smiled and handed over the hose then faced Ben and the lawyer again.

'James...died six months ago,' she managed. 'Of non-

Hodgkin's lymphoma.' Then she stopped again and stared across at the little girl fiercely watering tomatoes. She looked like she could find no words.

'So tell me about this child.' Ben still had his arms folded. The guy in the suit with his professional detachment in the face of such a situation was making him feel ill, but he glanced at Ginny again and knew he needed to keep hold of his temper. He needed facts. 'What's her full name?'

'I told you...Barbara Louise Carmody. Everything's in the case. All her paperwork. Get out of my way, please,' the lawyer snapped. 'I'm leaving.'

'Ginny...' Ben said urgently, but Ginny wasn't looking at him. Or at the lawyer. She was staring at the tiny, dark-eyed girl.

'This...this little girl broke my heart,' she whispered, and Ben suddenly figured it out. Or the bones of it. Her husband had fathered a child with someone else. She'd faced her husband's death, and now she was coping with betrayal as well as loss.

How could anyone expect her to accept this child? he wondered incredulously. How could she even bear to look at her? But she'd reacted to her with instinctive protectiveness. At such an age, with Down's, with a hose in her hand and plants to water, the hurtful words around the little girl would disappear.

But...*she'd said she'd take her. Indefinitely?*

'Do you have her medical records in her luggage?' Ginny asked, in a cold, dead voice.

'Of course,' the lawyer said smoothly. 'I told you. Everything's there.'

'Did you know she's Down's?' Ben demanded, and Ginny nodded.

'Yes, I did. I'm sorry, I should be more prepared. This is fine.' She took a deep breath, visibly hauling herself together. 'You can go,' she told the lawyer. 'You're right, the documentation can happen later. Thank you for bringing her to me. I regret I didn't receive the emails but I'd still rather have her here now than have her spend time in an institution.'

Then she stooped down and took the little girl's hands in hers, hose and all, and she met that long, serious gaze full on as the water sprayed sideways. And Ben saw the re-emergence of the Ginny he knew, the Ginny who faced challenges head on, his brave, funny Ginny who faced down the world.

'I was married to your...to your father,' she said. 'That means I'm your stepmum. If it's okay with you, Barbara, I'll look after you now. You can live with me. I need help watering all my plants. I need help doing all sorts of things. We might even have fun together. I'd like that and I hope you'll like it, too.'

CHAPTER TWO

THERE WAS NOTHING else Ben could think of to say. The lawyer climbed into his rental car and drove away. The car disappeared below the ridge, and the sound faded to nothing.

There was a long, long silence. Somewhere a plover was calling to its mate. The sea was a glistening backdrop, the soft hush-hush of the surf a whisper on the warm sea breeze.

Ginny's world had been fragmented and was now floating in pieces, Ben thought.

He thought of her blank refusal to practise medicine. He thought of the unknown husband's death. He thought of her accepting the responsibility for a child not hers, and he knew that fragmentation hadn't happened today. It was the result of past history he knew little about.

He'd hardly talked to her for years. He knew nothing of what had happened to her in the interim except the bare bones she'd told his mother when she'd returned to the island, but now she was kneeling beside the tomatoes, holding Barbara, looking bereft, and he felt his heart twist as... as Ginny had made his heart twist all those years before.

But now wasn't the time for emotion. He flipped open the child's suitcase and searched, fast. If the medical and legal stuff wasn't there he could still stop the lawyer from leaving the island.

But it was all there, a neat file detailing medical history, family history, lawyer's contacts, even contacts for the pre-school she'd been going to.

She might not have been loved but she'd been cared for, Ben thought grimly.

How could a family simply desert her?

'She has Mosaic Down's,' he said out loud, skimming through the medical history, and Ginny closed her eyes. She'd know what that meant, though. Mosaic Downs meant the faulty division of chromosomes had happened after fer-tilisation, meaning every cell wasn't necessarily affected.

But it was still bad. Barbara had the distinct look of Down's. Who knew what organs were affected?

Taking on a child was huge, Ben thought. Taking on a Down's child…

Barbara had gone back to watering. She was totally oc-cupied in directing the hose. They could talk.

They needed to talk.

'Ginny, are you serious?' he said urgently. 'I can still stop him.'

'And then what'll happen?' She shook herself. 'No. I'm sorry. I'm not handling this well. I did know this was com-ing. I did agree to this, even if it's happened sooner than I thought. I *will* look after her.'

'No one can ask that of you,' Ben said, and Ginny met his gaze head on. There was a long silence and then she gave a decisive nod, a gesture he remembered.

'No,' she said. 'They can't, but I will. Veronica and James did exactly what they wanted. Their selfishness was bound-less but there's no way this little one should suffer. James's death set me free, and Barbara should be free as well, not stuck in some institution for the disabled.' She managed to smile at the little girl—but then she felt silent again.

She was overwhelmed, Ben thought, and rightly so. Her world had just been turned on its head.

And Barbara? She was totally silent. She didn't look upset, though. She simply stood patiently watering, waiting for what came next.

Down's syndrome…

A man could mount arguments, Ben thought, for giving the whole human race Down's. Yes, it took Down's kids longer to learn things. Down's kids seldom reached average intellectual milestones, but, on the other hand, the Down's patients he had were friendly, selfless and desired little more than for those around them to be happy.

He walked forward and crouched beside Barbara. Ginny seemed almost incapable of speech. Maybe she'd said what she needed to say, and it was as if she didn't know where to go from here.

'Hi,' Ben said to the little girl. 'I'm Dr Ben.'

If he was right about this little one being well cared for, physically at least, then she'd be accustomed to doctors, he thought. Strange places would be associated with medical tests. Using the term 'doctor' might make this situation less strange.

And he was right. The little girl turned her gaze to him, but not to him personally. To his top pocket.

The arc of water went wild and no one cared.

'Jelly bean?' she said hopefully, and he grinned because some things were universal. Doctors' bribes.

'Jelly baby,' he said, and fished a yellow jelly baby from a packet in his shirt pocket. She took it gravely and then continued gazing at him—assessing him for more?

'Do you like jelly babies, Barbara?' he asked, and she frowned.

'Not…not Barbara,' she whispered.

'You're not Barbara?'

'Not Barbara,' she said, suddenly distressed. She looked down at her pink dress, dropped the hose and grabbed a button and pulled, as if trying to see it, as if trying to reassure herself it was still there. 'Button.'

'Button?' Ben repeated, and the little girl's face reacted as if a light had been turned on.

'Button,' she said in huge satisfaction, and Ben thought someone, somewhere—a nanny perhaps—had decided that Barbara was far too formal for this little girl, and Button it was.

'Your name is Button,' Ginny whispered, and Ben saw a wash of anger pass over her face. Real anger. Anger at her late husband and the unknown Veronica? He watched as she fought it down and tried for calm. 'Button, your mum's sent you to me so I can look after you. Maybe watering these to-matoes can wait. Would you like to come inside and have a glass of lemonade?'

'Yes,' Button said, and Ginny smiled. And then she looked uncertain.

'I have nothing,' she faltered. 'I really wasn't expecting her until next month. I don't know…'

'Tell you what,' Ben said, rising and dusting dirt from his knees. What was happening here was dramatic but he still had imperatives. Those imperatives had seen him take time out to try and persuade Ginny to be a doctor. That was a no go, especially now, but he still had at least twenty patients to see before he called it a day.

'You take Button inside and give her lemonade, then go through her suitcase and see what she has. When you have it sorted, bring her down to the clinic. I can give Button a good once-over—make sure everything's okay…'

'I can do that.'

'So you can,' he said. 'You're a doctor. Okay, forget the once-over. But our clinic nurse, Abby, has a five-year-old and she's a mum. If you don't need a doctor, you might need a mum to tell you all the things you're likely to need, to lend you any equipment you don't have. I have a child seat in the back of my Jeep—I use the Jeep for occasional patient transport. I'll leave it with you so you can bring Button down. I'll have Abby organise you another—the hire car place has seats they loan out.'

'I... Thank you.'

He hesitated, and once again he felt the surge of emotion he thought he'd long forgotten. Which was crazy. One long-ago love affair should make no difference to how he reacted to this woman now. 'Ginny, is this okay?' he demanded, trying to sound professionally caring—instead of personally caring. 'Are you sure you don't want me to ring Bob—he's the local cop—and have him drag the lawyer from the ferry?'

She looked at him then, really looked at him, and it was as if somehow what she saw gave her strength.

'No. I'm okay,' she said. 'I need to be. I don't have a choice and neither does Button. Thank you for your help, but we'll be fine.'

'You will bring her to the clinic?'

She hesitated. 'Yes,' she conceded at last.

'Big of you.'

She gave a faint smile. 'Sorry. I guess I'm not up for awards for good manners right now. But I am grateful. I'll come to the clinic when I need to. Thank you, Ben, and goodbye.'

She watched him go and she felt...desolate.

Desolate was how she'd been feeling for six months now. Or more.

Once upon a time her life had been under control. She was the indulged only daughter of wealthy, influential people. She was clever and she was sure of herself.

There'd been a tiny hiccup in her life when as a teenager

she'd thought she'd fallen in love with Ben McMahon, but even then she'd been enough in control to figure it out, to bow to her parents' dictates.

Sure, she'd thought Ben was gorgeous, but he was one of twelve kids, the son of the nanny her parents had hired to take care of her whenever they had been on the island. At seventeen she'd long outgrown the need for a nanny but she and Ben had stayed friends.

He had been her holiday romance, welcoming her with joy whenever her parents had come to the island, being her friend, sharing her first kiss, but he had been an escape from the real world, not a part of it.

His proposal that last year when they'd both finished school had been a shock, questioning whether her worlds could merge, and she'd known they couldn't. Her father had spelled that out in no uncertain terms.

Real life was the ambition her parents had instilled in her. Real life had been the circle she'd moved in in her prestigious girls' school.

Real life had become medicine, study, still the elite social life she'd shared with her parents' circle, then James, marriage, moving up the professional scale...

But even before James had been diagnosed with non-Hodgkin's lymphoma she'd known something had been dreadfully wrong. Or maybe she'd always known something had been wrong, she conceded. It was just that it had taken more courage than she'd had to admit it.

Then her father had died, dramatically, of a heart attack. She'd watched her mother, dry eyed at the funeral, already gathering the trappings of rich widow about her.

The night of the funeral James had had to go out. 'Work,' he'd said, and had kissed her perfunctorily. 'Go to bed, babe, and have a good cry. Cry and get over it.'

Like her mother, she hadn't cried either.

She'd thought that night… She'd known but she hadn't wanted to face it. If she worked hard enough, she didn't have to face it.

'Lemonade or raspberry cordial?' she asked Button. She sat her at the kitchen table and put lemonade in front of her and also the red cordial. Button looked at them both gravely and finally decided on red. Huge decision. Her relief at having made it almost made Ginny smile.

Almost.

She found herself remembering the day of James's funeral. It had been the end of a truly appalling time, when she'd fought with every ounce of her medical knowledge to keep him and yet nothing could hold him. He'd been angry for his entire illness, angry at his body for betraying him, at the medical profession that couldn't save him, but mostly at Ginny, who was healthy when he wasn't.

'—you, Florence Nightingale.' The crude swearing was the last thing he'd said to her, and she'd stood at his graveside and felt sick and cold and empty.

And then she'd grown aware of Veronica. Veronica was the wife of James's boss. She'd walked up to Ginny, ostensibly to hug her, but as she'd hugged, she'd whispered.

'You didn't lose him. You never had him in the first place. You and my husband were just the stage props for our life. What we had was fun, fantasy, everything life should be.'

And then Veronica's assumed face was back on, her wife-of-James's-boss mantle, and Ginny thought maybe she'd imagined it.

But then she'd read James's will.

'To my daughter, Barbara, to be held in trust by my wife, Guinevere, to be used at her discretion if Barbara's true parentage is ever discovered.'

She remembered a late-night conversation the week before James had died. She'd thought he was rambling.

'The kid. He thinks it's his. If he finds out...I'll do the right thing. Bloody kid should be in a home anyway. Do the right thing for me, babe. I know you will—you always do the right thing. Stupid cow.'

Was this just more? she thought, pouring a second glass for the obviously thirsty little girl. Guinevere doing the right thing. Guinevere being a stupid cow?

'I'm not Guinevere, I'm Ginny,' she said aloud, and her voice startled her, but she knew she was right.

Taking Button wasn't doing something for James or for Veronica or for anyone, she told herself. This was purely between *her* and Button.

They'd move on, together.

'Ginny,' Button said now, trying the name out for size, and Ginny sat at the table beside this tiny girl and tried to figure it out.

Ginny and Button.

Two of a kind? Two people thrown out of their worlds?

Only she hadn't been thrown. She'd walked away from medicine and she'd walked away from Sydney.

Her father had left her the vineyard. It had been a no-brainer to come here.

And Ben...

Was Ben the reason she'd come back here?

So many thoughts...

Ben's huge family. Twelve kids. She remembered the day her mother had dropped her off, aged all of eight. 'This woman's looking after you today, Guinevere,' she'd told her. 'Your father and I are playing golf. Be good.'

She'd got a hug from Ben's mother, a huge welcoming beam. 'Come on in, sweetheart, welcome to our muddle.'

She'd walked into the crowded jumble that had been their home and Ben had been at the stove, lifting the lid on pop-corn just as it popped.

Kernels were going everywhere, there were shouts of laughter and derision, the dogs were going nuts, the place was chaos. And eight-year-old Ben was smiling at her.

'Ever made popcorn? Want to give it a go? Reckon the dog's got this lot. And then I'll take you taddying.'

'Taddying?'

'Looking for tadpoles,' he'd said, and his eight-year-old eyes had gleamed with mischief. 'You're a real city slicker, aren't you?'

And despite what happened next—or maybe because of it—they'd been pretty much best friends from that moment.

She hadn't come back for Ben; she knew she hadn't, but maybe that was part of the pull that had brought her back to the island. Uncomplicated acceptance. Here she could lick her wounds in private. Figure out where she'd go from here.

Grow grapes?

With Button.

'We need to make you a bedroom,' she told Button, and the little girl's face grew suddenly grave.

'I want Monkey in my bedroom,' she said.

Monkey? Uh-oh.

She flipped open the little girl's suitcase. It was neatly packed—dresses, pyjamas, knickers, socks, shoes, coats. There was a file containing medical records and a small box labelled 'Medications'. She flipped this open and was relieved to find nothing more sinister than asthma medication.

But no monkey.

She remembered her mother's scorn from years ago as she'd belligerently packed her beloved Barny Bear to bring to the island.

'Leave that grubby thing at home, Guinevere. You have far nicer toys.'

'I want Monkey,' Button whispered again, and Ginny looked at her desolate little face and thought Button couldn't have fought as she had. Despite her mother's disgust, Ginny had brought Barny, and she'd loved him until he'd finally, tragically been chewed to bits by one of Ben's family's puppies.

But fighting for a soft toy wouldn't be in Button's skill range, she thought, and then she realised that's what she'd taken on from this moment. Fighting on Button's behalf.

She tried to remember now the sensations she'd felt when she'd received the lawyer's initial documents laying out why Button was being deserted by the people who'd cared for her. Rage? Disgust? Empathy?

This was a child no one wanted.

Taking her in had seemed like a good idea, even noble. Veronica and James had acted without morality. She'd make up for it, somehow.

Alone?

She was glad Ben had been here when Button had arrived. She sort of wanted him here now. He'd know how to cope with a missing Monkey.

Or not. Don't be a wimp, she told herself. You can do this. And then she thought, You don't have a choice.

But...he had offered to help.

'I guess you left Monkey at home,' she told Button, because there was no other explanation but the truth. 'I might be able to find someone who'll send him to us, but for now... let's have lunch and then we'll go down to Dr Ben's clinic. I don't have any monkeys here, but Dr Ben might know someone who does.'

Ben had told her the clinic would be busy but she'd had no concept of just how busy. There were people queued up through the waiting room and into the corridor beyond.

Plague? Ginny thought, but none of the people here looked

really ill. There were a few people looking wan amongst them but most looked in rude health.

She'd led Button into the reception area, but she took one look and tugged Button backwards. But as she did, an inner door swung open. Ben appeared, followed by a harassed-looking nurse.

Ben-the-doctor.

She'd seen him a couple of times since she'd returned to the island. She'd met him once in the main street where he'd greeted her with pleasure and she'd been calmly, deliberately pleasant. But dismissive. She'd returned to the island to get some peace, to learn about vineyards, but to treat the place as her parents had treated it—an escape. She'd had no intention of being sucked into island life.

Then this afternoon he'd asked her to help him—and then he'd helped her. She'd been incredibly grateful that he'd been there to face down the lawyer on her behalf.

But now he was facing, what, twenty patients, with one harried-looking nurse helping.

He looked competent, though, she thought, and then she thought, no, he looked more than competent.

At seventeen they'd shared their first kiss after a day's truly excellent surfing, and there had been a reason she'd thought she'd fallen in love with him. He'd been her best friend but he had been an awesome surfer, he'd been kind and…cute?

There was no way she'd describe Ben as cute now. Twelve years had filled out that lanky frame, had turned boy into man, and the man he'd become…

He was tall, lean, ripped. He had sun-bleached brown hair and sea-blue eyes. Did he still surf? He looked a bit weath-ered, so maybe he did. He was wearing chinos, a shirt and a tie, but the shirtsleeves were rolled up and the tie was a bit askew, as if he'd been working hard and was expecting more work to come.

He'd taken time out today to visit her. That was why the queue had built up, she thought, and then she thought taking time out must have been an act of desperation. He'd made himself later still in an attempt to get the help he desperately needed.

He was surrounded by need. He looked harassed to the point of exhaustion.

'Ginny,' he said flatly as he saw her, and then managed a smile. 'Hi, Button.' He sighed. 'Ginny, I need to spend some time with you and Button—I reckon she does need that check-up—but as you can see, I'm under pressure. Do you think you could come back in an hour or so? I hadn't expected you so soon.'

An hour or so. She looked around the waiting room and thought...an hour or so?

She knew this island. There was a solid fishing community, and there were always tourists, but there was also a fair proportion of retirees, escapees from the rat race of the mainland, so there were thus many elderly residents.

What was the bet that Ben would have half a dozen house calls lined up after clinic? she thought, and glanced at his face, saw the tension and knew she was right.

'Can I help?' she said, almost before she knew she intended to say it.

His face stilled. 'You said...'

'For this afternoon only,' she said flatly. 'But you helped me with Button.' As if that explained everything—which it didn't. 'If there's someone who could care for Button...'

'You're sure?' Ben's face stilled with surprise, but before she could speak he shook his head. 'Stupid, stupid, stupid. The lady's made the offer in front of witnesses.' And before she could speak again he'd knelt by Button. 'Button, do you like making chocolate cake?'

'Yes,' Button said, a response he was starting to expect. She was puzzled but game.

'This is Nurse Abby,' Ben said, motioning to the nurse beside him. 'Abby's little boy is making chocolate cupcakes with my sister, Hannah, right now. We have a kitchen right next door. When they're finished they'll decorate them with chocolate buttons and then walk down to the beach to have fish and chips for tea. Would you like to do that?'

'Yes,' she said again, and Ginny thought, God bless Down's kids, with their friendly, unquestioning outlook on the world. If Button had been a normal four-year-old, she'd no doubt be a ball of tension right now, and who'd blame her? But Down's kids tended to accept the world as they found it.

She would get her Monkey back for her, she thought fiercely, and she picked Button up and gave her a hug.

'You're such a good girl,' she said, and Button gave a pleased smile.

'I'm a good girl,' she said, and beamed, and Abby took her hand and led her out to where chocolate cupcakes were waiting and Ginny was left looking at Ben, while twenty-odd islanders looked on.

'Everyone, this is...' Ben hesitated. 'Dr Ginny Koestrel?'

'Yes,' she said, and turned to the room at large. She had no doubt what the islanders thought of her parents but she'd never changed her name and she had no intention of starting now.

'Many of you know my parents owned Red Fire Winery. You'll know Henry Stubbs—he's been looking after it for us, but he hasn't been well so I've come home to run it. But Ben's right, I'm a doctor. I'm an Australian and for this afternoon I'm here to help.' She took a deep breath, seeing myriad questions building.

Okay, she thought, if she was going to be a source of gossip, why not use it to advantage?

'Ben says many of you are just here for prescriptions,' she said. 'If you're happy to have an Aussie doctor, I can see you—we can get you all home earlier that way. I'll need to get scripts signed by Dr Ben because I don't have New Zealand accreditation yet, but I can check your records, make sure there are no problems, write the scripts and then Dr Ben can sign them in between seeing patients who need to see him for other reasons. Is that okay with everyone?'

It was. First, Ben's face cleared with relief and she knew she was right in thinking he had house calls lined up afterwards. Second, every face in the waiting room was looking at her with avid interest. Guinevere Koestrel, daughter of the millionaires who'd swanned around the island, splashing money around, but now not looking like a millionaire at all. She'd been on the island for months but she'd kept herself to herself. Now suddenly she was in the clinic with a little girl.

She knew there'd have been gossip circulating about her since her arrival. Here was a chance for that gossip to be confirmed in person. She could practically see patients who'd come with minor ailments swapping to the prescription-only side of the queue. She glanced at Ben and saw him grin and knew he was thinking exactly the same.

'Excellent plan, Dr Koestrel,' he said. He motioned to the door beside the one he'd just come out of. 'That's our second consulting suite. I'm sorry we don't have time for a tour. You want to go in there and make yourself comfortable? There's software on the computer that'll show pharmacy lists. I'll have Abby come in and show you around. She can do your patient histories, guide you through. Thank you very much,' he said. 'And you don't need to explain about Henry. Henry's here.'

He turned to an elderly man in the corner, and she realised with a shock that it was her farm manager.

Henry had been caretaker for her parents' vineyard for ever. It had been Henry's phone call—'Sorry, miss, but my arthritis is getting bad and you need to think about replacing me'—that had fed the impulse to return, but when she'd come he hadn't let her help. He'd simply wanted to be gone.

'I'm right, miss,' he'd said, clearing out the caretaker's residence and ignoring her protests that she'd like him to stay. 'I've got me own place. I'm done with Koestrels.'

Her parents had a lot to answer for, she thought savagely, realising how shabby the caretaker's residence had become, how badly the old man had been treated, and then she thought maybe she had a lot to answer for, too. At seventeen she'd been as sure of her place in the world as her parents—and just as oblivious of Henry's.

'This means I can see you next, Henry,' Ben said gently. 'We have Dr Ginny here now and suddenly life is a lot easier for all of us.'

She'd said that her help was for this afternoon only, but she had to stay.

Ben had no doubt she'd come to the clinic under pressure, but the fact that she'd seen the workload he was facing and had reacted was a good sign. Wasn't it?

It had to be. He had a qualified doctor working in the room next door and there was no way he was letting her go.

Even if it was Ginny Koestrel.

Especially if it was Ginny Koestrel?

See, there was a direction he didn't want his thoughts to take. She was simply a medical degree on legs, he told himself. She was a way to keep the islanders safe. Except she was Ginny.

He remembered the first time she'd come to the island.

Her parents had bought the vineyard when he'd been eight and they'd arrived that first summer with a houseful of guests. They'd been there to have fun, and they hadn't wanted to be bothered with their small daughter.

So they'd employed his mum and he'd been at the kitchen window when her parents had dropped her off. She'd been wearing a white pleated skirt and a pretty pink cardigan, her bright red hair had been arranged into two pretty pig-tails tied with matching pink ribbon, and she'd stood on the front lawn—or what the McMahons loosely termed front lawn—looking lost.

She was the daughter of rich summer visitors. He and his siblings had been prepared to scorn her. Their mum had taken in a few odd kids to earn extra money.

Mostly they had been nice to them, but he could remember his sister, Jacinta, saying scornfully, 'Well, we don't have to be nice to *her*. She can't be a millionaire and have friends like us, even if we offered.'

Jacinta had taken one look at the pleated skirt and pink cardigan and tilted her nose and taken off.

But Ben was the closest to her in age. 'Be nice to Guine-vere,' his mother had told him. He'd shown her how to make popcorn—and then he'd shown her how to catch tadpoles. White pleated skirt and all.

Yeah, well, he'd got into trouble over that but it had been worth it. They'd caught tadpoles, they'd spent the summer watching them turn into frogs and by the time they'd re-leased them the day before she'd returned to Sydney, they'd been inseparable.

One stupid hormonal summer at the end of it had inter-fered with the memory, but she was still Ginny at heart, he thought. She'd be able to teach Button to catch tadpoles.

Um…Henry. Henry was sitting beside him, waiting to talk about his indigestion.

'She's better'n her parents,' Henry said dubiously, and they both knew who he was talking about.

'She'd want to be. Her parents were horrors.'

'She wanted me to stay at the homestead,' he went on. 'For life, like. She wanted to fix the manager's house up. That was a nice gesture.'

'So why didn't you?'

'I have me dad's cottage out on the headland,' Henry said. 'It'll do me. And when I'm there I can forget about boss and employee. I can forget about rich and poor. Like you did when she were a kid.'

Until reality had taken over, Ben thought. Until he'd suggested their lives could collide.

Henry was right. Keep the worlds separate. He'd learned that at the age of seventeen and he wasn't going to forget it.

Think of her as rich.

Think of her as a woman who'd just been landed with a little girl called Button, a little girl who'd present all sorts of challenges and who she hadn't had to take. Think of Ginny's face when the lawyer had talked of dumping Button in an institution...

Think of Henry's indigestion.

'Have you been sticking only to the anti-inflammatories I've been prescribing?' he asked suspiciously. Henry had had hassles before when he'd topped up his prescription meds with over-the-counter pills.

'Course I have,' Henry said virtuously

Ben looked at him and thought, You're lying through your teeth. It was very tempting to pop another pill when you had pain, and he'd had trouble making Henry understand the difference between paracetamol—which was okay to take if you had a stomach ulcer—and ibuprofen—which wasn't.

Ginny...

No. Henry's stomach problems were right here, right now. That was what he had to think of.

He didn't need—or want—to think about Ginny Koestrel as any more than a colleague. A colleague and nothing more.

CHAPTER THREE

GINNY WORKED THROUGH until six. It was easy enough work, sifting through patient histories, checking that their requests for medication made sense, writing scripts, sending them out for Ben to countersign, but she was aware as she did it that this was the first step on a slippery slope into island life.

The islanders were fearful of an earthquake—sort of. Squid was preaching doom so they were taking precautions—buying candles, stocking the pantry, getting a decent supply of any medication they needed—but as Ginny worked she realised they weren't overwhelmingly afraid.

Earth tremors had been part of this country's history for ever. The islanders weren't so worried that they'd put aside the fact that Guinevere Koestler was treating them. This was Ginny, whose parents had swanned around the island for years and whose parents had treated islanders merely as a source of labour.

She hadn't been back since she'd been seventeen. Once she'd gone to medical school she'd found excuses not to accompany her parents on their summer vacations—to be honest, she'd found her parents' attitude increasingly distasteful. And then there had been this thing with Ben—so the islands were seeing her now for the first time as a grown-up Koestler.

The island grapevine was notorious. Every islander would

know by now that she'd been landed with a child, and every islander wanted to know more.

She fended off queries as best she could but even so, every consultation took three times longer than it should have and by the time she was done she was tired and worried about Button.

Button?

Where was she headed? She'd spent the last six months building herself a cocoon of isolation. One afternoon and it had been shattered.

She needed to rebuild, fast.

She took the last script out to the desk and Ben was waiting for her.

'All done,' she said. 'Mrs Grayson's cortisone ointment is the last.' She handed over the script she'd just written. 'This'll keep that eczema at bay until Christmas.'

He grinned and greeted Olive Grayson with wry good humour, signed the script and watched the lady depart.

The waiting room was empty. The receptionist was gone. There was no one but Ben.

'Button…' she started, and headed towards the kitchenette, but Ben put a hand on her shoulder and stopped her.

It shouldn't feel like this, she thought, suddenly breathless. Ben touching her?

For heaven's sake, she wasn't seventeen any more. Once upon a time she'd thought she was in love with this man. It had been adolescent nonsense and there was no reason for her hormones to go into overdrive now.

'I hope you don't mind but I sent her home with our nurse, Abby,' he said.

'You…what?'

'Abby's a single mum and the tremors happening when she can't be with her son are doing her head in. So my mum's taking a hand. Abby will be having dinner with us, so I suggested she and Hannah—my sister—take both kids back to our place. They'll have put them to bed, and dinner's waiting for us. Mum says there's plenty. I have a few house calls to make but they can wait until after dinner if you'd like to join us.'

'You...'

'I know, I'm an overbearing, manipulating toad,' he said, smiling. 'I've manipulated you into working for us this afternoon and now I've manipulated you into a dinner date. But it's not actually a dinner date in the romantic sense. It's Mum, Dad, whichever of my siblings are home tonight, Abby, Button and you. It's hardly candlelit seduction.'

She smiled back, but only just. This was exactly what she didn't want, being drawn into island life. She wanted to work on her vineyard. She wanted to forget about being a doctor. She wanted...

Nothing. She wanted nothing, nothing and nothing.

'Why not medicine?' Ben said softly, watching her face, and she thought almost hysterically that he always had been able to read her thoughts.

'What...what do you mean?'

'I mean I did some research when I heard you were back on the island. You've got yourself a fine medical degree. And yet...'

'And yet my husband died of cancer,' she said flatly, almost defiantly

'And there was nothing you could do? You blame yourself or your medicine? Is that it?'

'This is not your business.'

'But you walked away.'

'Leave it, Ben. I changed direction. I can't let the vineyard go to ruin.'

'We need a doctor here more than we need wine.'

'And I need wine more than I need medicine. Now, if you don't mind...I'll collect Button and go home.'

'My mum will be hurt if you don't stop and eat.'

She would be, too.

She'd popped in to see Ailsa when she'd arrived back at the island—of course she had. Ben's mum had always been lovely to her, drawing her into the family, making her time on the island so much better than if she'd been left with the normally sullen adolescent childminders her parents had usually hired on the mainland.

But she'd explained things to Ailsa.

'I need time to myself—to come to terms with my husband's death.' To come to terms with her husband's betrayal? His anger? His totally unjustified blame? 'I'm done with relationships, medicine, pressure. I need to be alone.'

'Of course you do, dear,' Ailsa had said, and had hugged her. 'But don't stay solitary too long. There's no better cure than hugs, and hugs are what you'll get when you come to this house. And if I know our kids and our friends, it won't only be me who'll be doing the hugging.'

Nothing had changed, she thought. This island was a time warp, the escape her parents had always treated it as.

She wanted this island but she didn't want the closeness that went with it. For six months she'd held herself aloof but now...

'Irish stew and parsley dumplings,' Ben said, grinning and putting on a nice, seductive face. His left eyebrow rose and he chuckled at her expression. 'Who needs candlelight and champagne when there's dumplings?' He held out his hands. 'Mum says it's your favourite.'

She'd remembered. Ailsa had remembered!

'And the kids are already sorting toys for Button,' he said, and tugged her toward the door. 'Come on home, Ginny.'

Home.

She didn't want to go. Every sense was screaming at her to go back to the vineyard.

But Button was asleep at Ailsa's. Ailsa had made parsley dumplings.

Ben was holding her hands and smiling at her.

What was a woman to do? A woman seemed to have no choice at all.

'Fine,' she said.

'That doesn't sound gracious,' he said, but still he smiled.

She caught herself. She was sounding like a brat.

'I'm sorry. It's very generous…'

'It's you who's generous,' he said gently. 'If you hadn't helped I wouldn't be getting any dinner, and Mum knows that as well as I do. So thank you, Ginny, and don't feel as if by coming you're beholden. Or even that you're somehow putting your feet into quicksand. You can draw back. You can go back to your vineyard and your solitude but not before you've eaten some of Mum's Irish stew.'

There were eight people around Ailsa's kitchen table, and the kids were asleep on the squishy living-room settee just through the door. The children were still in sight of the table. They were still part of the family.

It had always been thus, Ginny thought. Not only had Ailsa and her long-suffering Doug produced twelve children, but their house expanded to fit all comers. Doug worked on one of the island's fishing trawlers. He spent long times away at sea and when he was home he seemed content to sit by the fire, puffing an empty pipe.

'I know you smoke it at sea, but not in the house, not with the children,' Ailsa had decreed, and Doug didn't mind. He regarded his brood and Ailsa's strays with bemused approval and the house was the warmer for his presence.

Eight was a small tableful for these two, but the kids were

mostly grown now, setting up their own places. Ben was the third of twelve but only the three youngest were home to-night. Becky, Sam and Hannah were fourteen, fifteen and seventeen respectively, and they greeted Abby with warmth and shoved up to make room for her.

Abby, the nurse who'd worked with her that afternoon, was already there. The nurse had impressed Ginny today, not only with her people skills but with her warmth. She looked at home at the table, as if Ben often had her here.

Abby and Ben? A question started.

Ben was helping his mother ladle dumplings onto plates. Doug hardly said a word—it was up to the kids to do the entertaining, and they did.

'It's lovely to see you again,' seventeen-year-old Hannah said, a bit pink with teenage self-consciousness as she said it. 'We missed you when you went.'

'Ginny was Ben's girlfriend,' fourteen-year-old Becky told Abby, with no teenage self-consciousness at all. 'I'm too young to remember but everyone says they were all kissy-kissy. And then Ginny went away and Ben broke his heart.'

'Becky!' her family said, almost as one, and she flushed.

'Well, he did. Maureen said he did.'

Ginny remembered Maureen. Maureen was the oldest of the McMahon tribe, self-assertive and bossy. She'd come to see Ginny on the last night Ginny had been on the island, all those years ago.

'You could have been kind. Ben's so upset. You could say you'll write. Something like that.'

How to say that she couldn't bear to write? That even at seventeen all she'd wanted to do had been to fling herself into Ben's arms and stay? That she'd talked to her parents about the possibility of university in Auckland but she hadn't been able to divorce the request from the way she'd felt about Ben, and her parents had laid down an ultimatum.

'You're being ridiculous. The boy has no hope of making it through medicine—twelve kids—they're dirt poor. Cut it off now, Guinevere, if you want to be kind, otherwise you'll simply distract him from trying. You're going to university in Sydney and if there's any more nonsense, we'll send you to your aunt in London.'

The boy has no hope of making it through medicine. You'll simply distract him from trying.

The phrases had stung but even at seventeen she had been able to see the truth in them.

Ben had wanted so much to be a doctor. He'd dreamed of it, ached for it. Since he'd been fifteen he'd worked on the docks after school, unloading fish and cleaning them for sale. It was a filthy, hard job, and every cent of what he'd earned had gone to his doctor training fund.

You'll simply distract him from trying.

And then her father had issued another ultimatum, this one even worse.

Okay. If she couldn't study in Auckland... If she couldn't be with him...

She'd made a decision then and there, a Joan of Arc martyrdom, an adolescent burning for a cause. She'd renounce him and prove her parents wrong. She'd tell him not to write, to forget her, to focus purely on his career. Then, when they were both qualified doctors, she'd come again, appear out of the mist, probably wearing something white and floaty, and the orchestra would play and...and...

She found herself smiling, and everyone at the table was looking at her oddly. Even Ben.

'Sorry,' she said. 'I was just remembering how romantic it was. Our first love. I hope your heart wasn't broken for long, Ben.'

He grinned. 'For months,' he said.

'I thought you started going out with Daphne Harcourt

that same summer,' Hannah retorted. 'Now, *they* were kissy kissy. And then there was that painted one you brought home from uni.'

'And Jessica Crosby with the weird leggings and piercings,' Becky volunteered. 'She was hot. And now Mum thinks Abby—'

'Enough,' Doug said, breaking in abruptly. 'Leave the lad alone.'

They subsided as everyone always did when Doug spoke, and why wouldn't you subside when Ailsa's Irish stew was in front of you? But Ginny couldn't help thinking...thinking...

So Ben hadn't carried a flame for her. That was good, wasn't it? Yeah, it was, for of course at seventeen she hadn't carried a torch for him all that long either. She'd immersed herself in university life, she'd had a couple of very nice boyfriends, and then she'd met James.

He'd been older than her, his parents had moved in her parents' circle and he'd already been a qualified surgeon. She'd been thrilled when he'd noticed her, even more thrilled when he'd proposed.

And that same naivety that had had her dreaming of returning to Kaimotu in clouds of white mist with orchestra backing had then propelled her into a marriage that had been a disaster.

'Ginny,' Ben said gently, and she looked up and met his gaze. He looked concerned. Drat, he'd always been able to read her face and it was disconcerting. 'Are you okay? Did we work you too hard?'

'Would you like to stay here the night, with the little one?' Ailsa asked. 'Ben says you've been dropped into parenthood and it's hard. She's sound asleep now. She'll be right here.'

It was so tempting. She could step back into the McMahons' protection, she thought, as she'd stepped into it all those years ago.

Its warmth enfolded her. This family…

And then she glanced at Abby, who was looking fiercely down at her dinner plate, and she thought, What am I messing with? If there was something between these two, the kids talking of past loves must really hurt.

Joan of Arc syndrome again? Move aside, Ginny?

It wasn't dumb, though, she thought. There were no white mists and orchestras in the background now, just hard reality that had been drummed into her ever since she'd made her wedding vows.

'Thank you but no,' she managed. 'It's a lovely offer but Button and I will be fine.'

'I've put together a wee pack of toys for her,' Ailsa said. 'She likes Ben's old stuffed turtle, Shuffles.'

She flashed a glance at Ben at that, and then looked away fast. Noble doctor donating his Shuffles… It was dumb but why did that tug her heartstrings?

'Thank…thank you.'

'If there's anything else we can do…'

'I can babysit,' Hannah said. 'I'm supposed to be at uni but I copped glandular fever and missed the first two months of the semester. We figured it was best if I took the next two months off as well and start again at mid-year. So if you want to help Ben at the clinic I can keep helping out with Button. I…I do it for money,' she said, a trifle self-consciously. 'I mean…I'm sort of saving to be a doctor, too.'

'We'd love some help,' Ben said. 'Wouldn't we, Abby?'

'And you know, Ginny, it might help Button settle,' Ailsa said softly. 'She'll find it strange just the two of you. Ben seems to think she's been used to babysitters, so maybe stretching the care might help her adjust. Hannah looks after Abby's little boy, Jack, after school. The little ones played really well tonight. It might help you, too, and as Ben says, we need all the medical help we can get.'

They were all looking at her. The pressure...the pressure...

'No,' she said, and seven lots of eyebrows went up.

'Whoops, sorry,' she said, realising how petty her 'no' had sounded. 'It's just...'

'It's very fast,' Ailsa said, and came round the table to give her a hug. 'Ginny, we all know your husband died and we're very sorry. We should give you space. It's just...we know how hard Ben's pushed.'

'When I'm qualified, I can help,' Hannah said, and Ginny glanced at the girl and saw how much she meant it.

They all wanted to help—and she could.

'I'm sorry,' she managed. 'It's just...I can't.'

'Then you can't,' Ailsa said solidly, and glared at Ben. 'If she can't then she can't, so don't ask it of her. Ben, I know Ginny and I know she's been through a bad time. You're not to nag and you're to leave her alone until she's ready. Thank her very much for this afternoon and let her be.'

'Thank you very much for this afternoon,' Ben said gravely, and then he smiled at her.

It was the smile she remembered. It was the smile that had twisted her seventeen-year-old heart.

It was a white-mists-and-orchestra smile.

Enough.

She focussed on her dumplings and the talk started up again, cheerful banter as there always was around this table. As she'd always remembered.

People didn't look at her at this table. They didn't focus on her manners, they didn't demand she join in politely, they simply...were.

She glanced up and Ben was still watching her. His smile was faintly quizzical.

He wouldn't push. This whole community wouldn't push. They'd settle for what she was prepared to give.

How mean was it of her not to help?

She…couldn't.

'Call yourself a doctor… Stupid cow, you can't even give an injection without shaking…'

It wasn't true. She'd been okay until James…until James…

'Call yourself a doctor…'

'It's okay, Ginny,' Ben said gently. 'No pressure.'

She flushed and tried to look at him and couldn't. She'd been a doctor that afternoon, she told herself fiercely. Why couldn't she keep going?

Because Button needed her, she thought, and there was almost relief in the thought. In one day she'd become a step-mother. It was scary territory, but not as scary as stepping back into…life?

The chatter was starting up again around the table. No pressure.

This family was full of friends, she thought ruefully, and maybe…maybe that was what she needed. She could accept friendship.

Without giving anything in return?

It had to wait, she thought. If she said yes… If she got her New Zealand registration, she'd be expected to be a real doctor again.

'Call yourself a doctor…'

'No pressure at all,' Ailsa said gently beside her. 'The island can wait. Your friends can wait. We can all wait until you're ready.'

She smiled at Ginny, a warm, maternal smile.

Friends, Ginny thought, and tried to smile back. Friends felt…good.

So much for isolation, she decided as she tried to join in the cheerful banter around the table, but at least she'd left the white mists and orchestras behind her.

* * *

Ben walked her out to the car. He helped her buckle the sleeping Button into her newly acquired child seat, and then stood back and looked at her in the moonlight.

'We tried to blackmail you,' he said softly. 'The lawyer and then me. I'm sorry.'

'I… You didn't.'

'I manipulated you into helping this afternoon.'

'I did that all by myself.'

'Sort of,' he said wryly. 'I know how conscience works. Mrs Guttering met me in the supermarket last week and started complaining about her toe. Before I knew it she had her boots off and I was inspecting her ingrown toenail between the ice cream and frozen peas. How do you say no? I haven't learned yet.'

'And yet I have,' she said, trying to smile, trying to keep it light, as he had, and he put a hand out to cup her chin.

She flinched and moved back and he frowned.

'Ginny, it's okay. Saying no is your right.'

'Th-thank you.'

The lights were on inside. The kids were still around the table. Someone had turned the telly on and laughter sounded out through the window.

Kids. Home.

She glanced away from Ben, who was looking at her in concern. She looked into the car at Button and something inside her firmed. Button. Her stepdaughter.

Out of all of this mess—one true thing. She would focus on Button. Nothing else.

'You want her,' Ben said on a note of discovery, and she nodded, mutely.

What had she let herself in for? she thought, but she knew she wanted it. The moment she'd seen that clause in James's will…

When she and James had married, a baby had been high on her list of priorities, but James hadn't been keen. 'Let's put it on hold, babe, until our careers are established. The biological clock doesn't start winding down until thirty-five. We have years.'

But for Ginny, in a marriage that had been increasingly isolating, a baby had seemed a huge thing, something to love, something to hold, a reason to get up in the morning.

As medicine wasn't?

It should be, she thought. There'd never been a time when she hadn't thought she'd be a doctor. Her parents had expected it of her. She'd expected it of herself and she'd enjoyed her training.

She'd loved her first year as an intern, working in Accident and Emergency, helping people in the raw, but it had never been enough.

'Of course you'll specialise.' That had been her father, and James, too, of course, plus the increasingly ambitious circle of friends they'd moved in. 'You'd never just want to be a family doctor. You're far too good for that, Ginny.'

She was clever. She'd passed the exams. She'd been well on the way to qualifying in anaesthetics when James had got sick.

And after that life had been a blur—James's incredulity and anger that he of all people could be struck down, James searching for more and more interventionist cures, the medical fraternity around them fighting to the end.

'I should have frozen some sperm,' James had told her once, but she'd known he hadn't meant it—he'd never considered it. The idea that he was going to die had been inconceivable.

She'd watched as medical technology had taken her husband over, as he'd fought, fought, fought. She'd watched and experienced his fury. At the end he'd died undergoing yet another procedure, another intervention.

She remembered standing by his bedside at the end, thinking she would have liked to bring him here to this island, to have him die without tubes and interventions, to lie on the veranda and look out to sea...

James would have thought that was crazy.

'Can you tell me why you've decided to give up medicine?' Ben asked, and she shrugged.

'It couldn't save James.'

'Is that what you hoped? That you could save everyone?'

'No.'

'Then...'

'There was too much medicine,' she said flatly. 'Too much medicine and not enough love. I'm over it.'

'I'm sorry,' he said, as the silence stretched out and she stared out at the moonlight to the sea beyond—the sea was never far away on this island—and tried to figure where her life could go from here.

'We will find another doctor,' he said gently. 'This need is short term.'

'Are you still saying I should help?'

'I don't see why you can't. You were great today.'

'I need to look after Button.'

'That's not why you're refusing. You know it's not.'

'I don't need to give you any other reason.'

She looked into the back seat again, at the little girl curled into the child seat, sucking one thumb and hugging Ben's disreputable Shuffles with her spare arm. Ailsa and Abby had presented her with a dozen soft toys, from glossy teddies to pretty dolls, and Button had considered with care and gone straight for Ben's frayed turtle with one eye missing.

She looked like James, a little, and the thought was strange and unsettling, but even as she thought it Button wriggled further into her car seat and sighed and she thought, no, she looked like Button. She looked like herself and she'd go forward with no shadows at all. Please.

Ben was smiling a little, watching her watch Button hugging Shuffles. 'Mum never throws anything out.'

'You'd never have let her throw Shuffles out?' she asked incredulously, and amazingly he grinned, tension easing.

'Maybe not. Actually not. Over my dead body not.'

'Yet you let Button have him.'

'Button will love him as Shuffles needs to be loved,' he said, and then he looked at her—he really looked at her. 'Will you love her?' he said, and she stared at Button for a long, long moment and then gave a sharp, decisive nod.

'Yes.'

'And if her parents reclaim her?'

'They won't.'

'If they do?'

'Then I'll cope,' she said. 'Everyone copes. You know that. Like us thinking we were in love when we were seventeen. You move on.'

'Button needs a greater commitment than we were prepared to give,' he said, and she flushed.

'You think I don't know that?'

He gazed at her gravely, reading her face, seeing…what? How vulnerable she felt? How alone? How terrified to be landed with a little girl she knew nothing about?

Kids with Down's had medical problems to contend with, as well as learning difficulties. Heart problems, breathing problems, infections that turned nasty fast…

She'd cope. Out of all the mess that had been her relationship with James—his betrayal, his fury that she be the one to survive, his death—this little one was what was left.

James's death hadn't left her desolate but it had left her…

empty. Medicine was no longer a passion. Nothing was a passion.

If she could love this child…

But nothing else, she told herself fiercely. Nothing and no one else. She'd seen how fickle love was. Her parents' relationship had been a farce. James's professed love had been a lie, leading to bleakness and heartbreak. And even Ben… He'd said he loved her at seventeen but he'd found someone else that same summer.

'You moved on, too,' he said mildly, which brought her up with a jolt.

'Don't do that.'

'I don't know how not to,' he said obtusely, but she knew what he meant. That was the problem. She'd always guessed what he was going to say before he said it and it worked both ways.

'Then don't look at me,' she snapped, and then caught herself. 'Sorry. I didn't mean…'

'I know what you mean.

'Ben…'

He smiled wryly and held up his hands in surrender. 'Okay, I'm mentally closing my eyes here. Tomorrow afternoon, then? One o'clock?'

'No.'

'Ginny…'

'No!' She hesitated, feeling bad. Feeling trapped. 'In an emergency…'

'Isn't a host of panicked islanders an emergency?'

'Tell the islanders Squid has something obtuse like delusional encephalitis. Lock him in your quarantine ward until he starts prophesying untold riches instead of earthquakes.'

He grinned at that. 'It'd need back-up medical opinion to confine him. You'll sign the certificate?'

She smiled as well, but only faintly.

'I can't sign,' she said gently. 'I don't have New Zealand registration and I don't intend to get it.'

'Not if...?'

'No.'

He gazed at her for a long, long moment, reading her face, and she shifted from foot to foot under his gaze. He knew her too well, this man, and she didn't like it.

'Ginny, if I'd known you were having such an appalling time...' he said at last.

'I wasn't. Don't.'

'I should have written.'

'I told you not to.'

'And I listened,' he said obtusely. 'How dumb was that?' He shrugged. 'Well, you're home now. There's no need for letters, but I won't pressure you. I'll cope. Meanwhile, just see if you can open up a little. Let the island cure you.'

'I'm not broken. I've just...grown up, that's all.'

'Haven't we all,' he said, and his voice was suddenly deathly serious. 'Even Button. Cuddle her lots, Guinevere Koestrel, because growing up is hard to do.'

It was a night to think about but Ginny didn't think. She didn't think because she was so tired that by the time she hit the pillow her eyes closed all by themselves, and when she woke up a little hand was brushing through her hair, gently examining her.

It was morning and she was a mother.

She'd taken Button with her into her parents' big bed, fearful that the little girl would wake up and be afraid, but she didn't seem afraid.

She was playing with Ginny's hair and Ginny lay and let the sensations run through her, a tiny girl, unafraid, sleeping beside her, totally dependent on her, bemused by her mass of red curls.

She hadn't had a haircut since James had died—she hadn't been bothered—but now she thought she wouldn't. James had liked it cropped, but Ben...

She'd had long hair when Ben had known her. Ben had liked it long.

Ben...

It was strange, she thought. She'd been such good friends with Ben, but she'd barely thought of him for years.

She didn't want to think of him now. The sensations he engendered scared her. She'd fought so hard to be self-contained, and in one day...

It wasn't his fault she'd been landed with Button, she told herself, but she knew the sensations that scared her most had nothing to do with Button.

Button...Button was here and now. Button was her one true thing.

She found a brush and they took turns brushing each other's hair, a simple enough task but one Button found entrancing. Ginny enjoyed it, too, but she didn't enjoy it enough to stop thinking about Ben. To stop feeling guilty that she'd refused to help.

If she'd agreed... She wasn't sure about Australian doctors working in New Zealand but she suspected there'd be no problem. She might even be able to do more than write scripts.

She'd thought she wasn't missing medicine but yesterday, watching the diverse group of islanders come through her door, she'd thought...

She'd thought...

Maybe she shouldn't think, she told herself. The thing to do now was just whatever came next. It was her turn to brush Button's hair.

She brushed and it felt good. Making Button smile felt good. Sharing her home with this little girl felt....right.

She thought of last night, of Ailsa's table, and she thought homes were meant to hold more than one.

Button was winding her curls around her fingers. 'Red,' she said in satisfaction.

'Carrots,' she said, and Button considered—and then giggled.

'Carrots.'

Family, Ginny thought, and then suddenly found herself thinking of Abby, Ben's clinical nurse.

She seemed lovely. She was a single mum and a competent nurse. She worked beside Ben, and his parents obviously cared for her.

Good. Great, she told herself. It was lovely that he had a lady who was so obviously right for him.

Wasn't it?

Of course it was, she told herself harshly, and then it was her turn to brush so she needed to focus on something that wasn't Ben and Abby.

For there was no need to think of anything past Button and the vineyard.

No need at all.

Ben woke early and thought about Ginny. He should think about Abby, he told himself. His family had been matchmaking with every ounce of coercion they could manage. Abby was lovely. She was haunted a bit by her past but she was a gorgeous woman and a true friend.

As Ginny had been a friend?

See, there was the problem. One hot day in his eighteenth year Ben had stopped thinking of Ginny as a friend. They'd been surfing. It had been a sweltering day so there'd been no need for wetsuits. They'd waited, lying at the back of the swell for the perfect wave, and when it had come they'd caught it together.

They'd surfed in side by side, the perfect curve, power, beauty, translucent blue all around them.

The wave had sunk to nothing in the shallows and they'd sunk as well, rolling off their boards to lie in the shallows.

Her long, lithe body had touched his. Skin against skin...

He'd kissed her and he'd known he would never forget that kiss. It had him still wanting to touch her after all these years. Still unable to keep his hands away from her.

What he felt for Abby was friendship, pure and simple. But Ginny... Seeing her today, spending time with her, watching her care for Button...

Yeah, the hormones were still there.

Hormones, however, could be controlled. Must be controlled.

'There should be pills,' he told himself, and then thought there probably were.

Anti-love potions?

Except he didn't need them. It was true he'd got over his adolescent lust. He'd had other girlfriends, moved on.

Out of sight, out of mind? Definitely. He'd had a few very nice girlfriends. Nothing serious, but fun.

The problem was that Ginny wasn't out of sight now and the physical attraction had slammed straight back...

But the class thing still held true. He remembered that final night, in his shabby suit, Ginny dressed as if she'd just come off the Paris catwalks, and he remembered her gentle smile.

Impossible.

Yeah, so class, social standing had been important then, he told himself. Not so much now.

But then there were her ghosts. Big ones, he thought. A guy who'd betrayed her? A past that made her want to give up medicine? He didn't know it all. He could only guess.

If he wanted her...

What was he about, still wanting her?

He didn't, he told himself. This was nostalgia speaking, surely.

'Get over it,' he told himself harshly. 'She's rich, independent and wants nothing to do with you. She doesn't want to be a doctor any more and she can surely afford to do what she likes. It's her call. Leave her alone. One haunted society doctor who doesn't want to be a doctor at all—no and no and no.'

The week wore on.

Down on the docks, Squid's doomsday forebodings were increasing rather than fading.

'She'll be a big one. I'm telling you, she'll be a big one.'

Ben thought longingly of Ginny's suggestion of quarantine and locks and keys and thought he could almost justify it.

But despite Squid's doom-mongering, the islanders were calming down. They were growing accustomed to his prophecy; starting to laugh about it. The urgent medical need faded.

He received a couple of applications for doctors to take Catherine's place, but neither of them was prepared to come to the island for an interview. What sort of commitment was that? he thought, trying to figure out how he could find time to take the ferry to Auckland and interview them.

Maybe Ginny could help.

Maybe he couldn't ask her.

A couple of days after their dinner, she booked Button into the clinic, brought her in and together he and Ginny gave the little girl a complete medical assessment. That was weird, a mixture of personal and medical. It made him feel...

Like he didn't want to feel.

'You haven't changed your mind?' he asked, labelling

blood samples to send to the mainland for path. testing. He was…they both were…a bit concerned about Button's heart. Heart conditions were common in Down's kids. He thought he could hear a murmur. There was nothing about a murmur in her medical records but Ginny thought she could hear one, too.

'Button needs me,' she said simply, and it was true, but it worked both ways, he thought. He could see how much she cared for the little girl already.

He looked at them both, Button playing happily with Shuffles, calmly accepting his ministrations, seemingly unperturbed that her life had been turned upside down—and he looked at Ginny's pale, strained face.

'Maybe you need Button more than she needs you,' he said gently.

'No.'

'I won't go there, then,' he said equitably, and lifted Button from the examination couch and popped her on the floor. Ginny took her hand and backed away—almost as if she was afraid of him.

'I'll let you know when the results come through,' he said.

'Thank you.'

'Ginny…'

'Thank you,' she said again, and it was like a shield. Patient thanking doctor.

Nothing personal at all.

Once in the car she could block out the personal. Once out of sight of Ben.

She kind of liked taking Button home. No, more than liked. She was trying to hold back, aware at any minute that Veronica or Veronica's husband could change their mind and want her again, but Button was a little girl who was easy to love, and she found her heart twisting at the thought of her being discarded.

She might even fight for her, she thought. What rights did a stepmother have?

Maybe none, she thought, but there was a real possibility she'd be taking care of Button for life—and right now Button was filling a void. Button needed her and she intended to do the best job she could.

Which meant she was justified in refusing to help Ben, she decided, and squashed guilt to the back of her mind. One of her girlfriends had once told her, 'Don't have kids, Ginny. The moment you do, every single thing is your fault. No matter what you do, you feel guilty.'

So she was just like other mothers, she decided, and thought she should ring Ben up and tell him.

Or not.

Focus on Button. And the vineyard? She wasn't actually very good at growing grapes. She should find someone to replace Henry. She didn't actually have a clue what she was doing.

But, then, so what if she missed a harvest? she decided. The world had enough wine and she didn't need the money. Henry popped in to see her and worried about it on her behalf, but she calmed him.

'Next year, when I'm more organised, I'll hire staff and do it properly. I should have done it this year but neither of us was organised. And you're not well. Thank you for dropping by, but I'll manage. Did Ben…? Did Dr McMahon give you something that'll help?'

'He wants me to go to the mainland and have a gas-gastroscopy or something. Damned fool idea. You want me to teach you about—?'

'No,' she said gently, thinking of the old man's grey face.

'Let's put this year's harvest behind us and move on next year.'

That was a great idea, she decided. She'd put the whole of the last year aside. She'd refuse to be haunted by shadows of the past.

She and Button could make themselves a life here. She watched Button water her beloved tomatoes—watering was Button's principal pleasure—and thought…she could almost be happy.

But happiness was a long-ago concept. Pre-James.

Happiness went right back to Ben—and there was the biggie.

But why was it unsettling her? Once upon a time she'd thought of him as her best friend. Friends instead of lovers? Why not again?

He wanted her to do more. She could, she conceded. Hannah could look after Button.

Working side by side with Ben?

Why did she keep remembering one hot day in the surf?

Why did the memory scare her stupid?

CHAPTER FOUR

Running a solo practice was okay, was even feasible, except in emergencies.

With only ten beds, Kaimotu Hospital was not usually used for acute care. Acute-care cases were sent to the mainland, and now, with only one doctor, it was a case of deeming more cases acute.

With two doctors on the island they could cope with routine things like appendicitis, hernias, minor surgery, but with only one...well, the Hercules transport plane from the mainland got more of a workout.

The islanders hated it. They loathed being shipped to the mainland away from family and friends, but Ben had no choice. Until they found another doctor, this was the only way he could cope.

He did cope—until the night Henry's ulcer decided to perforate.

Why did medical emergencies happen in the small hours more often than not? Someone should write a thesis, Ben thought wearily, picking up the phone. His apartment was right by the hospital. He switched his phone through to the nurses' station while he slept, so he knew the nurse on call had overridden that switch. This call, therefore, meant he was needed.

'Ben?' It was Margy, the island's most senior nurse, and he knew the moment he heard her voice that he had trouble.

'Mmm?'

'Henry's on the phone. I'm putting you through now.'

'B-Ben?'

The old winemaker wasn't voluble at the best of times, but now his voice was scarcely a whisper.

'Yeah, Henry, it's me. Tell me what's wrong.'

'Me guts,' Henry whispered. 'Pain...been going on all night. Took them pills you gave me and then some more but nothing's stopping it and now...vomiting blood, Doc. Couple times. Lotta blood.'

To say his heart sank would be an understatement. He was already out of bed, reaching for his pants.

'You're at home? Up on the headland?'

'Y-yeah.'

'Okay, I want you to go back to bed and lie very still while I wake Max and Ella up,' he told him. Max and Ella were the nearest farmers to Henry's tiny cottage. 'They'll bring you down to the hospital. I reckon you might have bleeding from your stomach. It'll be quicker if they bring you here rather than me go there.'

Besides, he thought, he needed to set up Theatre. Call in nurses.

He needed to call on Ginny. Now.

'I might make a mess of their car,' Henry whispered, and Ben told Henry what he thought about messing up a car compared to getting him to hospital fast.

Then he rang Max and Ella and thanked God for good, solid farming neighbours who he knew would take no argument from Henry. There'd also be no tearing round corners on two wheels.

Then he rang Ginny.

* * *

Ginny was curled up in her parents' big bed, cuddling a sleeping Button—and thinking about Ben.

Why did he keep her awake at night?

He didn't, she conceded. Everything kept her awake at night.

Memories of James. Memories of blame.

'You stupid cow, how the hell can you possibly know how I feel? You're healthy—healthy!—and you stand there acting sorry for me, and you can't do a thing. Why can't you get this damned syringe driver to work? How can you sleep when I'm in pain?'

The syringe driver *had* been working. It wasn't pain, she thought. It was fear, and fury. He'd had twelve months of illness and he'd blamed her every moment of the way.

So what was she doing, lying in bed now and thinking of another man? Thinking of another relationship?

She wasn't, she told herself fiercely. She was never going there again. She was just...thinking about everything, as she always did.

And then the phone rang.

She answered it before Button could wake up.

'Ginny?'

Ben's voice did things to her. It always had.

No.

'Ben?'

'Ginny, I need you. Henry has a ruptured stomach ulcer. He's been bleeding for hours. There's no time to evacuate him to the mainland. Mum and Hannah are on their way to your place now to take care of Button. The minute they get there I need you to come. Please.'

And that was that.

No choice.

She should say no, she thought desperately. She should tell him she'd made the decision not to practise medicine.

Not possible.

Henry.

'I'll come.'

'Ginny?'

'Yes?

'How are you at anaesthetics?'

'That's what I am,' she said, and then corrected herself. 'That's what I was. An anaesthetist.'

There was a moment's stunned silence. Then... 'Praise be,' Ben said simply. 'I'll have everything ready. Let's see if we can pull off a miracle.'

Henry needed a miracle. He'd been bleeding for hours.

Ginny walked into Theatre, took one look and her heart sank. She'd seen enough patients who'd bled out to know she was looking at someone who was close.

Ben had already set up IV lines, saline, plasma.

'I've cross-matched,' he said as she walked through the door. 'Thank God he's O-positive. We have enough.'

There was no time for personal. That one glance at Henry had told her there was hardly time for anything.

She moved to the sink to scrub, her eyes roving around the small theatre as she washed. He had everything at the ready. A middle-aged nurse was setting up equipment—Margy? Abby was there, slashing away clothing.

Ben had Henry's hand.

'Ginny's here,' he told him, and Ginny wondered if the old man was conscious enough to take it in. 'Your Ginny.'

'My Ginny,' he whispered, and he reached out and touched her arm.

'I'm here for you,' she told him, stooping so she was sure he'd hear. 'I'm here for you, Henry. You know I'm a doctor.

I'm an anaesthetist and I'm about to give you a something to send you to sleep. We need to do something about that pain. Ben and I are planning on fixing you, Henry, so is it okay if you go to sleep now?'

'Yes,' Henry whispered. 'You and Ben…I always thought you'd be a pair. Who'd a thought… You and Ben…'

And he drifted into unconsciousness.

She was an anaesthetist. *Who'd a thought?* Henry's words echoed through Ben's head as he worked and it was like a mantra.

Who'd a thought? A trained anaesthetist, right here when he needed her most.

Ben had done his first part of surgery before he'd returned to the island. It had seemed sensible—this place was remote and bad things happened fast. He'd also spent an intense six months delivering babies, but if he'd tried to train in every specialty he'd never have got back to Kaimotu.

Catherine had had basic anaesthetic training, as had the old doctor she'd replaced. For cases needing higher skills they'd depended on phone links with specialists on the mainland. It hadn't been perfect but it had been the best they could do.

Now, as he watched Ginny gently reassure Henry, as he watched her check dosage, slip the anaesthetic into the IV line he'd set up, as he watched her seamlessly turn to the breathing apparatus, checking the drips as she went to make sure there was no blockage in the lines, he thought… He thought Henry might just have a chance.

Henry had deteriorated since Ben had phoned Ginny. By the time Ginny had walked into Theatre he'd thought he'd lose him. Now…

'Go,' Ginny said, with a tight, professional nod, and she

went back to monitoring breathing, checking flow, keeping this old man alive, while Ben...

Ben exposed and sutured an ulcer?

It sounded easy. It wasn't.

He was trained in surgery but he didn't do it every day. He operated but he took his time, but now there was no time to take.

He cut, searched, while Margy swabbed. There was so much blood! Trying to locate the source of the bleeding...

'One on each side,' Ginny snapped to the nurses and they rearranged themselves fast. Ben hadn't had time to think about it but the way they had been positioned only Margy had been able to swab, with Abby preparing equipment.

'I can do the handling as well,' Ginny said calmly. 'Get that wound clear for Dr McMahon. Fast and light. Move.'

They moved and all of a sudden Ben could see...

A massive ulcer, oozing blood from the stomach wall.

That Henry wasn't dead already was a miracle.

'Sutures,' he said, and they were in his hand. He glanced up—just a glance—in time to see that it was Ginny who was preparing the sutures. And monitoring breathing, oxygen saturation, plasma flow.

No time to think about that now. Stitch.

Somehow he pulled the thing together, carefully, carefully, always conscious that pulling too tight, too fast could extend the wound rather than seal it.

The blood flow was easing.

How fast was Ginny getting that plasma in?

He glanced up at her again for a fraction of a moment and got a tiny, almost imperceptible nod for his pains.

'Oxygen saturation ninety-three. We're holding,' she said. 'If you want to do a bit of pretty embroidery in there, I think we can hold the canvas steady.'

And she'd taken the tension out of the room, just like that.

He and both the nurses there had trained in large city hospitals. They'd worked in theatres where complex, fraught surgery took place and they knew the banter that went on between professionals at the top of their game.

Ginny's one comment had somehow turned this tiny island hospital into the equal of those huge theatres.

They had the skill to do this and they all knew it.

'Henry's dog's name's Banjo,' Margy offered. They were all still working, hard, fast, not letting anything slide, but that fractional lessening of tension had helped them all. 'We could tell him we've embroidered "Banjo" on his innards when he wakes up.'

'He'd need *some* mirror to see it,' Ben retorted, and went back to stitching, but he was smiling and he had it sealed now. That Henry had held on for this long…

'Oxygen level's rising,' Ginny said. 'That's the first point rise. We're aiming for full within half an hour, people. Margy, can you find me more plasma?'

And Margy could because suddenly there was only the need for one to swab. Ben was stitching the outer walls of the stomach closed then the layers of muscle, carefully, painstakingly. Ginny was still doing her hawk thing—the anaesthetist was the last person in the room to relax—but this was going to be okay.

But then… 'Hold,' Ginny said into the stillness. 'No, hold. No!'

No!

They'd been so close. So close but not close enough. Ben didn't need to see the monitors to interpret Ginny's message—he had it in full.

A drop in blood pressure. Ventricular fibrillation.

He was grabbing patches from Margy, thanking God that at least the bulk of the stitching was done, but not actually thanking God yet. Saying a few words in his direction, more like.

Or one word.

Please... To get so close and then lose him...

Please...

The adrenaline was pumping. If Ginny hadn't been here...

Please...

'Back,' Ginny snapped, as he had the patches in place, as he moved to flick a switch...

A jerk... Henry's body seemed to stiffen—and then the thin blue line started up again, up and down, a nice steady beat, as if it had just stopped for a wee nap and was starting again better than ever.

'Oh, my God,' Margy said, and started to cry.

Margy and Henry's daughter had been friends before they'd both moved to the mainland, Ben remembered. That was the problem with this island. Everyone knew everyone.

'Every man's death diminishes me.' How much more so on an island as small as Kaimotu?

'He... I think he'll be okay,' Ginny said, and Ben cast her an anxious glance as well. Henry had worked for her parents for ever. Did she consider him a friend? The tremor in her voice said that she did.

'We'll settle him and transfer,' Ben said, forcing his hands to be steady, forcing his own heartbeat to settle. 'I want him in Coronary Care in Auckland.'

'He won't want that,' Margy said.

'Then we transfer him while he doesn't have the strength to argue,' Ben said. 'I'm fond of this old guy, too, and he's getting the best, whether he likes it or not. Thank God for Ginny. Thank God for defibrillators. And thank God for specialist cardiac physicians and gastroenterologists on the mainland, because if we can keep him alive until morning, that's where he's going.'

* * *

It was an hour later when he finished up. Henry seemed to have settled. Margy had hauled in extra nursing staff so he could have constant obs all night. Ben had done as much as he could. It was too risky to transfer Henry to the mainland tonight but he'd organised it for first thing in the morning. With his apartment so close he was just through the wall if he was needed.

Enough.

He'd sent Ginny home half an hour ago, but he walked out into the moonlight, to walk the few hundred yards to the specially built doctors' quarters, and Ginny was sitting on the rail dividing the car park from the road beyond. Just sitting in the moonlight.

Waiting for him?

'Hey,' she said, and shoved up a little on the rail to make room for him.

'Hey, yourself,' he said, feeling…weird. 'Why aren't you at home?'

'You reckon I could sleep?'

'I reckon you should sleep. What you did was awesome.'

'You were pretty awesome yourself. I didn't know you were surgically trained.'

'And I didn't know you'd done anaesthesia.'

'Once we were friends,' she said softly into the night. 'We should have kept up. I should have written. I should have let you write. One stupid summer and it meant we cut our friendship off at the knees.'

'As I recall,' he said carefully, 'it was a very nice summer.'

'It was,' she said, and smiled. 'We had fun.'

'You were the best tadpole catcher I ever knew.'

'I'm going to teach Button,' she said, and he wanted to say he would help but it wasn't wise. He knew it wasn't wise. She was opening up a little just by being here, and he wouldn't push for the world.

Except…he needed to ask.

'Why did you give up medicine?' he asked into the still-ness, and the night grew even more still.

'You know,' she said at last, 'that when the world gets crazy, when there are things around that are battering down in every direction, a tortoise retreats into his shell and stays there. I guess…that's what I've done.'

'Your shell being this island.'

'That's the one.'

'But medicine?'

'While James was dying… We tried everything and I mean everything. Every specialist, every treatment, every last scientific breakthrough. None of it helped.'

'You blame medicine?'

'No,' she said wearily. 'But I thought… My dad pushed and pushed me to do medicine and James pushed me to specialise, and when both of them were in trouble…Dad and then James…they both turned. They were so angry and there was nothing I could do. I used to go to bed at night and lie there and dream of being… I don't know…a filler-up of potholes. A gardener. A wine-maker. Something that made it not my fault.'

'It wasn't your fault your dad and James died.'

'No,' she said bleakly. 'But you try telling them that.'

'They're dead, Ginny.'

'Yes, but they're still on my shoulder. A daughter and a wife who didn't come up to standard.'

'That's nuts,' he said, and put a hand on her shoulder. He felt her stiffen.

'No,' she said.

'So you've rejected medicine because of them. You're re-jecting friendship, too?'

There was a long silence while they both sat and stared out over the moonlit sea. He kept his hand where it was, gently on her shoulder, and he felt her make a huge—vast—effort to relax.

What had those guys done to her—her father and her husband? He thought back to the laughing, carefree girl who'd been his friend and he felt...

Yeah, well, there was no use going down that road. He couldn't slug dead people.

He wanted to pull her closer. It took an almost superhuman effort to keep it light, hold the illusion that this was friendship, nothing more.

'I'll come out eventually,' Ginny said at last. 'I can't stay in my shell for ever and Button will haul me out faster.'

'You'll go back to the mainland?'

'No!' It was a fierce exclamation.

'This island's not for hiding, Ginny,' he said softly. 'Life happens here as well.'

'Yes, but I can take Button tadpoling here.'

'She'll love it.' He hesitated but the urge was too great. 'Let me in a little,' he said. 'We used to be friends. I'm the second-best tadpoler on the island. We could...share.'

She stiffened again. 'Ben, I don't... I can't...'

'Share?'

'That's the one.' She rose, brushing away his touch. Her face was pale in the moonlight and he wondered again what those guys had done to her. Unbidden he felt his hands clench into fists. His beautiful Ginny...

'It's okay,' he made himself say, forcing the anger from his voice. 'Treat the island as a shell, then. You have Button in there with you, though, and I have a feeling she'll tug you out. And you came out tonight. Henry's alive because you came out, and you can't imagine how grateful I am.'

'It's me who should be grateful,' she said. 'Henry was my friend.'

'Henry *is* your friend.' And then, as she didn't reply, he pushed a little bit further.

'Ginny, no one on this island judged you because of who your parents were. You stayed here for ten summers and there are lots of islanders who'd call you their friend. My family almost considered you one of us. We're all still here, Ginny, waiting for you to emerge and be our friend again.'

'I can't.'

'No,' he said, and because he couldn't stop himself he touched her cheek, a feather touch, because the need to touch her was irresistible and she was so beautiful and fearful and needful.

So Ginny.

'You can't,' he said. 'But tonight you did.' And then, before he knew what he was going to do, before she could possibly know for he hadn't even realised he was about to do it himself, he stooped and kissed her, lightly, on the lips.

It had been a feather touch. He'd backed away before she'd even realised he'd done it, appalled with himself, putting space between them, moving away before she could react with the fear he knew was in her.

But he had to say it.

'We're all here, waiting,' he said into the darkness. 'We'll wait for as long as it takes. This island is as old as time itself and it has all the patience in the world.'

And as if on cue the world trembled.

It was the faintest of earth tremors, exactly the same as the tremors that had shaken this island since time immemorial.

A tiny grumble of discord from within.

Nothing to worry about? Surely not.

'Or maybe it's saying hurry up,' Ben said, and grinned, and Ginny managed a shaky smile.

'It'll have to wait.'

'Maybe the island's giving you a nudge. Like we gave you a nudge. You saved Henry tonight, Ginny, so there's a start. No pressure, love, but when you come out of your shell, we're all waiting.'

No pressure.

He watched as she put her fingers to the lips he'd just kissed. He watched as she watched him, as something fought within her.

What had her father and husband done to her?

'I...I need to go,' she faltered, and he didn't move towards her and God only knew the effort it cost him not to.

'Yes, you do.'

'Ben...'

'Don't say anything more,' he said softly. 'You've done brilliantly tonight. I love what you're doing with Button— we all do. One step at a time, our Ginny, that's all we ask.'

He tugged open the door of her car and watched as she climbed in.

He didn't touch her and it almost killed him.

'Goodnight, Ginny,' he said softly, and she didn't say a thing in reply.

He stood back as she did up her seat belt, as she started the engine, as she drove away, and he thought...

She looks haunted.

Not by him, he thought. She needed time.

He would give her time. Except for emergencies. Even knowing she was on the island, another doctor...

Who was he kidding? Even knowing she was on the island...his Ginny.

He would give her time. He had to.

She reached the vineyard. The lights were on inside the house. Ailsa and Hannah would be there, keeping watch over Button, waiting for her, anxious about Henry.

This island was like a cocoon, she thought, a warm, safe blanket that enveloped her and kept her safe from the real world.

Did she ever need to go back to the real world?

Kaimotu was time out, a holiday isle, a place of escape.

She could make it real.

But if she did, would the world move in?

She thought back to her marriage. The fairy-tale. A big, gorgeous, clever man her parents had approved of, dating her, making love to her, making her feel like the princess in a fairy-tale. She could have her parents' life. She could have a happy-ever-after.

Yes, she'd had a childhood romance with Ben but that had been years before. She'd felt that what she'd found with James had been real, wonderful, a grown-up happy-ever-after.

And she'd stepped into James's world and realised that grown up wasn't fantasy. Not one little bit. Grown up was trying to meet expectations, climbing the career ladder, accepting scorn when you failed.

Grown up was realising that medicine couldn't save lives—that you could do nothing to help your father or your husband.

Grown up was learning to hate yourself as well as copping hate from those around you.

'I need a shrink,' she said out loud, and then closed her eyes, took a deep breath, stared up at the starlit sky and figured she didn't need a psychiatrist. She needed to move on. Move forward.

But not very much, and certainly not in the direction of Ben.

Ben had kissed her.

Ben was real.

No. He'd be just the same as all the other fantasies, she

told herself. She no longer trusted her judgement. She no longer trusted men who told her she was capable, beautiful, wonderful.

She no longer trusted.

'My job is to take care of Button and to make wine,' she told herself, and thought that actually she hadn't managed very well in the picking and processing department and there wouldn't be all that much Chardonnay coming out of the vineyard this season.

'It doesn't matter,' she said stubbornly. 'Button's the important thing.' Like Henry was important. She'd helped save Henry.

Yes, but for how long? He'd have another coronary, he'd arrest, he'd die and she'd feel…she'd feel…

'I'm not going to feel,' she said savagely into the dark. 'If Ben's desperate I'll help but nothing else. I will not be responsible for anything else but Button. It won't be my fault.'

'That's a cop-out and you know it,' she told herself, and she bit her lip and turned resolutely towards the house.

'I know it is,' she told herself. 'But it's all I'm capable of. And if Ben McMahon thinks he can change my mind just by kissing me… Pigs might fly, Ben McMahon, but you are not stuffing with my life.'

Sleep was nowhere. Ben lay in the dark and stared at the ceiling and all he could think about was that kiss.

He'd wanted her when he'd been seventeen, and he wanted her still. Crazy or not, his body was reacting to her as it had at seventeen.

He wanted her.

But while he wanted her as a woman, as the desire he'd felt all those years ago surged back to the surface, he needed her as a doctor. The skill she'd shown had knocked him sideways. He had to persuade her to join him; with her skills the island could have the medical service it deserved.

All sorts of possibilities had opened up as he'd watched her work. Islanders with cancer pain often needed to be transported to the mainland, at a time when they most wanted to stay here. He didn't have the skills to help them.

As an anaesthetist, Ginny had those skills.

So…was he messing with that need by making it personal? By letting his desire hold sway? He'd kissed her and she'd shied away like a frightened colt.

'So don't kiss her,' he said out loud, knowing that was easier said than done.

She'd been injured by the men in her life, he thought. She'd been injured by the arrogant bully he remembered her father being, and a husband who sounded like a bottom feeder. Ben wasn't seeing her as a victim, though. With her determination to keep Button, with the skill and humour she'd shown in Theatre tonight, he knew that underneath the battered armour there was still the lovely, feisty, carrot-haired girl he'd fallen in love with all those years ago.

'It was an adolescent crush,' he growled to the night. 'Get over it.'

But an adolescent crush wasn't what he was feeling. When his mouth had touched hers, a fire had reignited.

For her, too?

If it had, she wasn't letting on. Her armour might be battered but it was still intact, and if he wanted any chance at all of persuading her to work with him, he needed to respect it.

'So leave her be.'

'Except to ask her to work?' He was arguing out loud with himself.

'Yes,' he told himself. 'She worked that first afternoon because she saw desperate need. She worked tonight for the same reason. At the moment she's giving you back-up when you most need it. Respect that, give her space, give her time.'

'But the way you feel?'

'Get over it,' he said harshly. 'You're not seventeen any more. Go find yourself a lady who wants you.'

'And isn't that the whole trouble?' he groaned, and punched a pillow. This island was small, and any affair he had, even asking someone on a date, led to expectations and complications.

Like tonight. One kiss…

Expectations and complications?

'Leave it alone,' he growled, and punched the pillow once more then gave up and got up and went across to the hospital to check on Henry—who was sleeping soundly and didn't need his attention at all.

He went back to bed and finally he slept, but when he slept he dreamed of Ginny.

She was an adolescent crush who'd turned into the woman of his dreams. The idea was romantic nonsense, he told himself, even in his sleep.

And down on the harbour… It was five in the morning and almost every islander was asleep, but Squid Davies was wide awake and pacing.

'It's coming,' he muttered. 'The big one's coming. I feel it in my bones.' He grabbed a piece of paper and started to write.

'Just in case,' he muttered. 'I'll be prepared even if they're not.'

CHAPTER FIVE

BEN DIDN'T SEE Ginny for days.

Henry spent four days in hospital in Auckland and then was transferred back to the island. Ben heard from his mum that Ginny had tried to persuade the old man to come back to the vineyard and stay with her, but Henry wanted to go back to his ancient cottage on the headland. It was too far from anywhere, he thought. He wouldn't mind talking to Ginny about it.

'But Ginny's doing all she can,' Ailsa told him. 'She's visiting him twice a day. There's nothing more she can do. There's nothing more anyone can do.'

So he didn't have an exc—a reason to talk to her. But finally Button's cardiac results came through.

There'd been a query on Button's medical records, tests taken but not recorded. Her family doctor had noted that slight heart murmur, he'd sent her to a specialist but then she'd been brought to the island and the notes she'd brought hadn't contained results.

It had taken a week's perseverance on Ben's part to get them. Laws protecting a patient's privacy were a concern, especially when the patient was four years old, one parent had disappeared to Europe and the other wanted nothing to do with her. Ben had run out of professional ways of getting the results and had finally reverted to the personal. He'd rung

Veronica's husband, a man who blustered about not wanting anything to do with a child who wasn't his but at least didn't hang up on him.

'For now you're still legally Barbara's parent,' Ben had snapped at him. 'I'm now her doctor, Ginny's her acting guardian until the legalities are completed and we need full access to her medical records. Do you want her to die of heart failure because of your pride?'

The man had finally complied, and when Ben eventually received the results he swore.

There were problems. They'd have to be sorted. He and Ginny had to talk.

It was Monday, a gorgeous autumn day. Ben did a long morning's clinic then he needed to make some house calls, and Ginny's house was first.

He'd just reached the vineyard gate when the earth moved.

One moment Ginny was supervising Button eating her boiled egg and toast. The next moment she was on the floor and the world was crazy.

It was as if the whole house had been picked up and was being violently shaken. Walls became floor, floor became walls. Furniture was crashing everywhere.

She grabbed a chair but the chair slid sideways, crashed, rolled, tumbled.

Button!

She was screaming. Was Button screaming? The noise was unbelievable.

Somehow she grabbed the little girl as the chair she'd been sitting on crashed almost on top of her. She scooped her into her arms, and then the floor seemed to roll again.

The table. The table!

Drop and hold. Where had she heard that? In some long-ago safety lecture, maybe here in New Zealand when she'd been a child? New Zealand was known as the shaky isles for good reason.

There was another mantra. Get out of the house. Into the open.

But it was no use thinking that now, or trying to attempt it. This was like a wild, bucking, funfair ride, only there was nothing fun about this. Everything that wasn't nailed down was crashing around them.

She had Button cradled hard against her but she was struggling to hold her. She was fighting to stay on her knees.

The table… If she could get past these crazy chairs…

The table was big, solid, farmhouse wood. If she could get under…

Getting anywhere was impossible. Something sharp hit her head, and she thought, Drop further.

She dropped onto her side, ignoring the crunch of things breaking under her. Button was clinging to her, limpet-like, whimpering in terror, and Ginny could move where she wanted and she knew Button wouldn't let go.

Move where she wanted? That was a joke.

The table. She was three feet away. Roll. Roll!

The floor lurched again, tipping the other way, and under she went. She crashed into chair legs as she rolled but Button was with her, clinging so hard that Ginny had a hand free.

Grab.

She grabbed a table leg and clung.

She was under the table. The world was still rolling in great, fearsome waves, but the table and the floor beneath it were rolling with it and Ginny could hold and ride.

Thank God the house was single-storey, Ginny thought as she clung. And had an iron roof. No vast bank of heavy tiles.

Visions of knife-sharp iron flooded her mind but she

shoved them away. Just hold on. Use her body to protect Button and hold on.

Wait until the earth found a new level.

Ben was just about to turn into the gate when the road buckled.

As buckles went it was truly impressive. The coast road was long and flat, and he saw the buckle start half a mile ahead of him, rising with a massive, unbelievable heave of solid earth. It hurled towards him, a great, burrowing mound, trees swaying, bitumen cracking and falling away, coming, coming...

It must have been seconds only before the great buckling mound hit him but he had enough time to think about getting out of the car and then to change his mind and decide to stay in the car but veer away fast from trees, head for the grassy verge away from the sea, pull to a halt. Or almost pull to a halt for then it hit and the car rose in the air as if it had been thrown.

It wasn't just the one wave. It was a series of massive jolting, shaking heaves, as if the world was shifting and not knowing where to settle.

He gripped the steering-wheel and hung on. It was all he had to hold onto—the car was like a bucking bronco.

Oh, God, his island.

And stunningly, even while he was holding on for dear life, he felt himself switch into doctor mode. Earthquake. Casualties. This was major.

Squid had been right. Never doubt the sages, he thought, and then he stopped thinking because he had to hold tight and nothing else could matter.

The car rolled—it almost rolled right over—and then, unbelievably, it rolled back again, righting itself with a massive thump.

What sort of power…? What sort of damage…?

Tsunami.

The vision crashed into his mind with sickening dread. Earthquake, tsunami. Get to high land.

Not yet. He could do nothing yet but hold on.

His seat belt was holding him safe—sort of. He was fine, short of the cliff caving in and his car sliding into the sea…

Not a lot of use thinking that.

Hold on. There was nothing he could do until the rolling stopped.

But he was still thinking medicine.

Casualties. He hardly dared think but already he knew the islanders were in real trouble.

One doctor.

No, two. First things first. He'd grab Ginny.

Please, God, she was okay.

Don't go there. He glanced towards the house and saw it heave and shift on its foundations. Please, hold.

He'd get Ginny, take her back to the hospital, leave Button with his mother…

His parents. The kids.

Do not go there.

Plan instead. The earth was settling. Panic was turning to focus.

He'd call the mainland, get help organised. Maybe he could do it now.

He flicked his phone. He had a signal.

And then he didn't.

The telecommunications tower at the airport must have toppled.

No phone.

The authorities on the mainland would figure it out anyway, he thought grimly. A quake this size would show on every seismograph in the world.

He had two nurses on duty at the hospital, with six more on call. How many could get there?

Roads would be cut.

Roads... How...?

The car jerked and bucked and his grip on the wheel tightened.

Ginny, he thought. Please.

He stopped planning. He held on like grim death and he said the word over and over and over.

Please.

It went on and on and on. Just when she thought it had ended it started up again. She couldn't move—she daren't. Yes, the safest place was outside but to get there she'd have to negotiate her way through the house. There were massive exposed beams in the historic homestead. She was terrified of those beams and the table was midway between two of them so she was staying right where she was.

Button was amazingly calm. She clung and clung, and didn't say a word as they lay huddled under the massive table.

Weirdly, Ginny found herself singing, odd little nursery rhymes she'd heard from nannies as a child, and sometimes she heard Button add a word or two as well.

There was nothing and no one but the two of them and this table. The vineyard was miles from the nearest neighbour. The shaking went on.

She held Button, she clung to her table leg and she'd never felt so alone in her life.

One part of Ben was totally focussed on what was happening, seeing the cracks open in the road, watching parts of the cliff fall into the sea, watching Ginny's house buckle and sway.

One part of him was moving on, thinking tsunami warn-

ings, casualty centres, evacuation plans, emergency re-
sources.

The hospital was on high ground. It was weatherboard,
and watching Ginny's house he thought weatherboard was
the way to go.

But one of Ginny's chimneys had crashed.

Please…

Don't go there.

The ground was settling now, the massive undulations
passing. Any minute now he'd dare to get out of the car.

And go see if Ginny was safe.

The thought of her inside, near that crashed chimney,
made him feel ill.

But… It wasn't that he was especially worried about
Ginny, he told himself. It was just because she was here, now.
He'd watched her house heave—of course he was worried.

Plus she'd been part of his childhood. A friend.

But he knew there was more.

What were the levels of love?

It was hardly the time to think about that now. Finally the
world was ceasing to shake.

Maybe it was worst on this side of the island, he prayed.
Here the roads were buckled beyond using. Here huge trees
had crashed. Here Ginny's house…

Was still standing. He could see broken windows and
tumbled masonry. He thought suddenly of those massive
beams above the kitchen and the thought had him out of
the car and running before the earth had completely settled.

Ginny.

She should take Button out from under the table.

She was afraid to move.

The quake seemed to have passed. There were still tremors, but minor ones. She could venture out from under her table and make a run for outside.

She didn't want to. Here seemed the only safe place.

She stayed under her table and she held the silent Button and she hugged and hugged.

'It's okay, it's over,' she whispered, but she barely believed it.

'Ginny?'

The voice came from nowhere. No, it didn't, it came from the back veranda.

'Ben?' She could scarcely believe it. Ben! Here!

'Where are you?' he yelled.

'I-in the kitchen. Under the table. But the beams…'

She didn't finish. There was a series of crashes, like a bull moving through her living room, but maybe it was one desperate doctor hauling away the litter of damaged furniture blocking his path.

And then, unbelievably, he was under the table with her. He was gathering her—and Button—into his arms and he was holding them.

He held and held and her world changed yet again.

She'd thought it was over, but just as she pulled away a little, just as she relaxed and thought the world was settling, that Ben was here, that they were safe, another tremor hit.

It wasn't nearly as big as that first, vast wave, but it was big enough for Button to cling, for Ben to haul them both close again, for her to cling back.

And think again.

What she'd just thought.

Which was nonsense. Which was everything she'd vowed never to think again.

Safe in the arms of someone who loved her?

Life was a travesty, she thought as she clung, because she

still needed to cling, for Button's sake as well as her own. Button was cocooned between them, safe, protected by their bodies, a Button sandwich between her two protective adults.

Button needed Ben.

For now Ginny needed Ben—but just for now. Only for now, she told herself fiercely.

This was crazy. This was an earthquake, for heaven's sake, so why was she suddenly thinking of James, of a marriage that had made her glow, had made her think this was happy-ever-after, had made her believe in the fairy-tale?

Why was she thinking of the travesty that marriage had turned out to be? Of infidelity, of shattered trust. Of anger, more, of hatred, that she was the one to live. Of the knowledge that her judgement was appalling, that trust was stupid, that love was for the pages of fairy-tales.

'Ginny…'

'Mmm.' It seemed almost wrong to speak, as if somehow voices might stir the demons to shake some more.

'We need to get outside.'

'I think I like my table.'

'I like your table, too,' he said. 'But there's the little matter of beams above us. We can't depend on them falling straight if this gets any worse. We need to risk it. Button, we're going to run. We're going to wriggle out from under here, I'm going to carry you, because I'm stronger and faster than Ginny…'

'Ginny,' Button said, and clung tighter.

'I can see Shuffles,' Ben said, lightly now, making it seem almost conversational. 'He's right by the door on the floor. If you let me carry you, we'll rescue Shuffles and take him outside.

Button considered. There was silence while they let her make up her mind and then she gave a decisive nod.

She turned within their sandwich squeeze and transferred her hold to Ben.

'Get Shuffles,' she ordered. 'Go.'

'Yes, ma'am,' Ben said, and touched Ginny's face—just fleetingly, but she felt herself flinch.

He gave her a sharp, questioning glance but the time for questions wasn't now.

'Let's go,' he said, and hauled himself backwards from under the table, holding Button and Button holding him, and there was nothing left for Ginny to do but follow.

Outside was weird.

It was as if a giant hand had picked up and shaken the house, leaving its contents a vast, jumbled mess. Outside it almost looked normal.

The veranda steps had cracked and fallen sideways. The downpipes were hanging at crazy angles, windows were broken and a chimney had crumpled. Otherwise you might almost look at it and think nothing had happened.

'Old and weatherboard,' Ben said. They'd scrambled out of the house, moving fast in case another tremor hit, but now they were in the yard between house and stables, with no trees close, nothing but open ground. There was a deep crack running across the width of the yard, a foot wide, heaven knew how deep, but they were well clear of it.

'Wooden houses seem to stand up to quakes much better than brick,' Ben said. 'Thank God most of the island houses are wooden.'

He turned and stared towards the town and Ginny could see his mind turning to imperatives. Medical imperatives? Plus the fact that his parents and siblings were in the valley.

'Tsunami,' he said, and just as he said it a siren started, loud and screeching, blaring a warning. Even as a child here Ginny had learned what it meant.

What Ben had just said.

'It's too close,' she whispered.

'What?'

'I did a project at school. Tsunamis come when quakes happen out to sea. This one was so big…surely the fault's right under us.'

'Let's not bet our lives on it,' Ben said grimly. 'Get in the Jeep, now.'

'I can—'

'Get in the Jeep or I'll throw you in,' he said grimly, and he grabbed her hand with his free one—he was still cradling Button with the other—and ran across the yard.

Seconds later they were bucketing across the paddocks, heading up the steep valley incline. Fences were ignored—Ben simply steered his battered Jeep between the posts and crashed straight through.

Tsunami.

The word was enough to block out everything else. She held Button tightly—Ben had obviously decided he wasn't wasting precious seconds fastening her into her child seat—and stared down at the sea. Willing it to be okay.

Willing a wave not to come.

It didn't. They reached the ridge above the vineyard and stopped, then climbed from the Jeep and watched the sea while the siren still wailed across the island.

Ben produced field glasses from the Jeep and his expression grew more and more grim as he surveyed what he could of the island.

Ginny didn't ask to see. She didn't want to see. She held Button and she thought this was a hiatus. The last moment before reality.

She thought suddenly of the day she and James had gone to the hospital for him to get tests. They'd been practically sure but not…not prepared. Did anything prepare you for such a thing?

The tests were run. 'Come back at six and get the results,'

the oncologist had said, so they'd gone to the beach, swum, had a picnic, talked of everything under the sun until it was time to go back.

'If I'm okay we'll even have a baby,' she remembered James saying.

And she remembered thinking, Please, let this time not end.

Knowing that it would.

She was still watching the sea. Waiting for the world to end?

Ben was jabbing at his cell phone then turning his field glasses toward the island's small airport.

'The tower must be down,' he said, staring at the screen. 'I hoped it was just a glitch during the shake but everything's dead. We should be able to see the tower from here. There's no reception.'

Ginny hauled her phone out of her back jeans pocket and stared. No bars. Nothing.

'Oh, God,' she whispered.

'It'll be okay,' Ben said, and she saw the way he hauled himself under control. What lay before them might well be appalling. For him to be the only doctor… 'The guys on the fishing boats have radios that'll reach the mainland. A quake this big will be sensed from there. I'm guessing we'll get help fast.' His eyes roved over the island, noting signs of damage that from up here seemed small but she knew that once they got close it could spell calamity. 'Choppers can get here fast. An hour to scramble, two hours for the flight…'

'They'll come?'

'If they can't contact the hospital they'll come anyway. Hell, Ginny, I need to be there.' He winced as the siren kept on wailing and Ginny wondered whether if he wasn't saddled with Button and with her, he would have gone now, tsunami threat or not.

'If the coast road's out...we'll go overland as soon as the siren stops,' Ben said grimly, his field glasses sweeping slowly across the valley again. 'The coast road won't be safe. It'll be rough but the Jeep should do it.

'What...what's a few fences?' she said unsteadily, and Ben managed a smile.

'I hear the local landowner shoots trespassers on sight. Risks are everywhere.'

The local landowner would be her. She managed a smile back. 'You might be granted dispensation.'

'Dispensation. Wow!' And then his smile died. 'Ginny, will you help?'

'Of course I will.'

'No, *really* help,' he said. 'No holds barred. We'll need to leave Button with Hannah, as long as Hannah...' He broke off and went back to staring through his glasses and Ginny followed his line of sight and thought he'd be staring at an old wooden house in the middle of town that held his mum and dad and siblings.

'I think the hospital's intact. It's on high ground overlooking the harbour. It looks solid. I hope to hell our equipment's safe,' Ben said.

Ginny nodded. Ben needed to think of medical imperatives, she thought, or any imperatives rather than thinking about family, friends, for a quake of this magnitude had to mean casualties on a massive scale.

'Your family will be okay,' she said stoutly. 'Your house is as old and sturdy as mine, and your kitchen table's bigger. And I'm thinking your mum's the one who taught me about diving under it.'

'And Mum was preparing lamb roast for dinner tonight,' Ben managed. 'I hope she's taken the spuds under there with her. She should be peeling them now.'

She grinned, and then hugged him because she knew how

hard it had been to joke—and then she pulled away because there was no way she wanted him to think a hug meant anything but a hug.

'Ginny,' he said, and put a hand to her face, and for the life of her she couldn't stop herself flinching again.

Why did she flinch? Of all the stupid… Wasn't it about time she learned some control?

There was a moment's loaded pause, a silence broken only by the wail of the siren. For a long, long moment Ben gazed down at her, as if he was seeing right inside her.

'What did that *bastard* do to you?' he asked at last.

No. One minute they'd been talking earthquake, thinking earthquake, feeling earthquake, and the next…this?

She stared at him, stunned to stupefaction. She didn't want him to see. She didn't want anyone to see.

'I won't hurt you, Ginny,' Ben said gently, and he touched her face again. 'How can you think I will?'

She shook her head. This was crazy. There was no way she was answering that, here, now, or at any time.

She'd made a vow. Life on her terms, now and for ever.

As long as this shaking world permitted.

'Of course I'll help at the hospital,' she said, far too quickly.

'Good,' he said, and moved his field glasses on. But she knew he wouldn't be deflected. He knew her, this man, like no other person had ever known her—and the thought was terrifying.

She went back to hugging Button. Apart from the siren, it was incredibly peaceful. It was a gorgeous autumn afternoon. The sun was sinking low on the horizon and the grass underfoot was lush and green.

But there were cattle in the paddocks, and every beast had its head up. Because of the siren?

Um...no. Because the earth had just shifted and neither man nor beast knew what would happen next.

And then the siren stopped.

Ben's field glasses swung around until he found what he was looking for.

'We send the siren out from four points of the island,' he said slowly, thinking it through as he spoke. 'The sirens are set off from the seismology centre on the mainland. They're supposedly quake-proof and they get their signal via satellite. If they've stopped we can assume that boffins somewhere have decided there will be no tsunami. Thank God.'

'Thank God,' she repeated, and once again she got an odd look, the knowledge that he saw more than she wanted him to see. Earthquake or not, she knew now that there was a world of stuff between them, and she also knew it was stuff he'd hunt down until it was in the open.

'It's okay, Ginny,' he said gently. 'We can work side by side, I promise. This is professional only. We treat it as such. We go see what the damage is and how best we can start putting things back together again. And we put everything else aside until later.'

CHAPTER SIX

ON TOP OF everything else, she was fearful for her farm manager. Henry now lived on the headland beyond the vineyard, on his own.

'His place is so remote. Ben, we need to check…'

'We can't,' he said, as gently as he could manage. 'Henry's four miles that way overland, the coast road'll be cut and we'll have casualties coming into the hospital now. Ginny, I'm sorry, but triage says hospital first. We have to get to town.'

She knew he was right but it didn't make her feel better. Her car was a sedan, not capable of going cross-country. Ben's Jeep was their only mode of transport. They needed to travel together and there was only one direction they could head.

Henry was on his own and it made her feel ill. How many islanders were on their own?

They headed down the valley. It sounded simple. It wasn't.

Driving itself was straightforward enough. Ben had wire cutters in the Jeep, so if they came to a troublesome fence they simply cut the wires. The ground was scattered with newly torn furrows where the earth had been torn apart, but the Jeep was sturdy and Ben was competent.

Ginny thought they'd get back to the hospital fast, and then they crossed the next ridge and her nearest neighbours came into view. Caroline and Harold Barton. Caroline was sitting by a pile of rubble—a collapsed chimney—and she was sobbing.

'He went back in to try and get the cat,' she sobbed. 'I can't get the bricks off him. And the crazy thing is...' she motioned to a large ginger tom sunning himself obliviously on a pile of scattered firewood '...Hoover's fine. Oh, Harold...'

There was a moan from underneath the bricks and then an oath.

'Would you like to stop reporting on the bloody cat and get these bricks off me?' Harold's voice was healthily furious.

Ben lifted Button from the Jeep and handed her over to the sobbing lady.

'Button, this is Mrs Barton and she's crying because she's had a fright,' he said matter-of-factly. 'But now she's going to introduce you to her cat. Caroline, your job is to keep Button happy. Ginny, how are you at heaving bricks?'

'Fine,' Ginny said, knowing how desperate Ben was to get to the hospital but knowing they had no choice but to help the hapless Harold.

Ten minutes later they had him uncovered and, miraculously, his injuries were minor.

'Felt the bloody thing heave so I dived straight into the cavity itself,' he said. 'It could'a gone either way, on top of me or around me, so I was bloody lucky.'

He was, Ginny thought as Ben cleaned a gaping gash on his arm and pulled it together with steri-strips. It'd need stitching but stitching had to wait. The important thing to do now was stop the bleeding and move on.

Triage. The hospital. What was happening down in the town?

Bricks had fallen on Harold's leg as well. 'There's possibly a break,' Ben said, but Harold waved him away.

'Yeah, and you might be needed for something a bit more major than a possible ankle break. Caroline can put me on the tractor and we'll make our way down to town in our own good time. With the cat. With this ankle I'm not even going to be able to kick him so there's not a lot of choice. Get yourself down to those who need you, Doc.' And then he turned to Ginny. 'But thank God you came home when you did, girl. When you were a kid we always reckoned you belonged here. Seems we were right. You've come home just in time.'

They passed three more houses, with three more groups of frightened islanders. They crammed two women, three kids and two dogs into the back. There was nothing wrong with them except scratches and bruises, but they were all stranded and they wanted, desperately, to be in town with community support.

'I'm hoping someone's set up a refuge,' Ben said tightly to Ginny. 'I need to be there.'

He couldn't be there, though. At the next farmhouse they came to, an entire stone barn had collapsed. Once again they found a sobbing woman but there was no humour about this situation. One of the women distracted the kids while the rest grimly heaved stone. The elderly farmer must have been killed instantly.

They left old Donald Martin wrapped in a makeshift shroud, they tucked Flora into the front of the Jeep, and Flora sobbed all the way to the village—and hugged Button.

Button was amazing, Ginny thought. She was medicine all by herself. She even put her arms around this woman she'd never met before and cuddled her and said, 'Don't cry, lady, don't cry,' whereupon Flora sobbed harder and held her tighter. A normal four-year-old would have backed away in fear but Button just cuddled and held her as Ben pushed the loaded Jeep closer to town.

He was desperate, Ginny thought. The hospital, the whole

town was currently without a doctor. It was now almost five hours since the quake. They'd seen a couple of helicopters come in to land and Ben had relaxed a little bit—'Help must be coming from the mainland.'—but she could still see the tension lines on his face. Why wasn't he at the hospital?

If he hadn't been calling in on her... If he hadn't been bringing Button's test results...

'Ben, I'm so sorry,' she told him from the back seat, and Ben swivelled and gave her a hard stare before going back to concentrate on getting the Jeep across the next paddock.

'There's no fault,' he said grimly. 'Cut it out, Ginny, because I won't wear your guilt on top of everything else. I don't have time for it.'

And that put her in her place.

It was self-indulgent, she conceded, to think of guilt. She was crammed between two buxom women. She had kids draped over her knees.

Ben didn't have time to think about guilt, she thought, and then they entered the main street and neither did she.

The first things they saw were road cones. Orange witches' hats were stretched across the main street, forcing them to stop.

The light was fading but they could see the outlines of the buildings. They could see devastation.

Porches of old, heritage-style shopfronts had come crashing down. A car parked at the kerbside was half-buried under bricks and stones—and maybe it was more than one car, Ginny thought, gazing further along the road.

Right near where they'd been forced to stop, the front of Wilkinson's General Store had fallen away. So had the front of Miss Wilkinson's apartment upstairs. The elderly spinster's bedroom lay ripped open as if a can opener had zipped along the edge. Her bedroom, with chenille bedspread, her dressing gown hanging on the internal door, her teddy bears spread across the bed, was on view for all to see.

She'd be mortified, Ginny thought, appalled for the gentile old lady. And then she thought, Please, God, that she's safe enough to feel mortified.

There were no lights. At this time of day the streetlights should be flickering on, but instead the scene was descending into darkness.

A soldier was approaching them from the other side of the road block. A soldier?

Ben had the Jeep's window down, staring at this uniformed stranger in dismay. For heaven's sake, the man even had a gun!

'The main street's been declared a red zone,' the soldier stated. 'It's too dangerous to proceed. My orders are to keep everyone out.'

'I'm needed at the hospital on the other side of town,' Ben said with icy calm, and Ginny felt like reaching out from the back seat, touching him, reassuring him—but there was no reassurance to be had. 'I'm a doctor,' he said. 'I have people here who need treatment.'

'Sorry, sir, you still need to follow protocol,' the soldier said. 'You can pull the car to the side of the road—as far away from the rubble as you can, sir, and report to Incident Control Headquarters.'

'Incident Control Headquarters?' Ginny demanded, because Ben seemed almost speechless. She could see where his head was. Soldiers coming in and taking control of his island? 'Where exactly is Incident Control Headquarters?'

'Um…it's the tourist information centre,' the soldier said, unbending a little.

'Thank you,' Ben said tightly, and parked the Jeep, and he and Ginny ushered his tight little group of frightened citizens round the back of the shattered buildings towards the sounds and bustle and lights of…Incident Control Headquarters?

Here there were people everywhere. Floodlights lit the outside of what was normally tourist central. Serious men and women Ginny didn't recognise, wearing hard hats and bright orange overalls, were spilling in and out.

Ginny was clutching Button and holding Flora's hand with the hand she had spare. She was feeling ill. Ben was carrying two of the toddlers they'd brought down from the ridge, and he looked as grim as she felt.

It was almost five hours since the quake had hit, and what five hours ago had been a peaceful island setting had now been transformed. These people represented professional disaster management, she thought. They'd have been brought in by the choppers they'd seen.

Kaimotu Island must now be officially a disaster scene.

And then there was Abby, flying down the steps to meet them. Abby was also wearing orange overalls and a hard hat. A grim-faced man came behind her, obviously keeping her in sight, but Abby had eyes only for Ben.

'Ben—oh, thank God you're okay,' the nurse said. 'I've been so worried. Where have you been? We've been going out of our minds. Your mum—'

'She's okay?' Ben snapped, and Ginny had a further inkling of what he'd been going through. What he still was going through.

'She's fine,' Abby said hurriedly. 'As far as I know, all your family is okay. Doug's out with the searchers. Your house is intact and your mum and Hannah have set it up as a crèche.'

'Flora!' It was a cry from inside the hall. A group of ladies was dispensing sandwiches. One of these ladies darted forward and Ginny realised with relief that it was Daphne Hayward, Flora's sister.

And then she thought, irrelevantly, I know these people. I haven't been near this island for twelve years but I know them.

I'm one of them?

'Can you clear the entrance, please?' a soldier asked, and they all turned round and glared at him, Ginny, too, and Ginny thought incredulously, I'm an islander.

And then Ben lifted Button from her arms and she let her be lifted because it was the natural thing to do, to let Ben help her.

Ben. Her friend.

Her island, in trouble.

'Why aren't you at the hospital?' Ben was asking Abby as he hugged Button close. 'Who's in charge there?'

'Things are as under control as they can be,' Abby said, but her voice was tight and strained. Really tight and strained. 'We've had four choppers arrive containing emergency personnel, including two doctors. Margy's doing triage, and every nurse on the island's with her. One of the helicopters has already evacuated Percy Lockhart and Ivy Malone—both have serious crush injuries. One of the doctors is a surgeon. He's reducing a compound fracture now—Mary Richardson's arm. It's bad, Ben, it's really bad.'

Her voice faltered and she motioned to the grim-faced man behind her. 'This is Tom Kendrick. I... We know each other. He's with Search and Rescue from the mainland. We've been out. They wanted a nurse who knew people. I... I...'

The stranger behind Abby moved in closer, and Ginny saw his arm go round her waist. That was odd, she thought, but Ben was standing really close to Ginny, and she was sort of leaning against him. In fact, her own arm was suddenly round Ben. It was because she needed contact with Button, she told herself, but she knew it was more.

She wanted contact with Ben, and if Abby needed contact with this stranger…it sort of gave her permission to ask for contact herself.

But even as she thought it, she looked at Abby's face, she saw the lines of strain and fear—and suddenly she got it.

'Abby, where's Jack? Where's your son?'

'On…on the bus,' Abby whispered. 'We've just come back to get the chopper. Tom's organising a drop of blankets and food.'

'What the…?' Ben started.

'It's okay,' Tom reassured him, solid, professional, assured. 'We had a tense time for a while when we couldn't locate the school bus but we have it now. One of the fishing boats has seen it from the sea. It's trapped on the coast road round past the mines at the back of the island. There's been two landslips and the bus is trapped between them. As far as we know, they're all fine, but we're not going to be able to get them out until morning. Hence the airdrop. We'll drop a radio in as well.'

'So it'll be okay,' Abby said, still in that tight, strained voice, and Ginny wondered what else was wrong. But she had to move on. They all had to move on.

'They need you at the hospital,' Abby said, forcing her voice to sound almost normal. 'Here's Hannah— Ginny, is it okay if Button goes with her? You and Ginny are needed for medical stuff. Please, go fast. There are so many casualties. But Tom and I need to go now. We need this food drop done before it's completely dark. Tom, let's go.'

New Zealand was set up for earthquakes. Emergency services stood ready twenty-four hours a day. It had been years since there'd been a major quake but that didn't mean they'd relaxed.

The personnel who'd arrived were moving with clinical precision. As Ben and Ginny walked through the almost abandoned town, skirting damaged buildings, they saw teams moving silently from house to house, quickly checking, in some cases with dogs by their sides, making sure everyone was out and then doing lightning assessments of each building.

Using spray paint. Numbers. Colours or degrees of risk. Miss Wilkinson's general store came under the 'Do Not Approach Under Any Circumstances' heading and Ginny thought bleakly of those little pink teddies and a dignified old lady having to bunk down in the school hall tonight without her dressing gown and her pink friends.

Ben was holding her hand. Ginny hardly realised it, but when she did she didn't pull away.

This was too big to quibble. If Ben needed reassurance...

She even managed a slight smile at that. Who was she kidding? Her hold on his hand tightened and he gave her a reassuring smile in the dark.

'We'll get through this.'

'Oi!' It was a soldier, one of the many patrolling the streets. 'You guys need to get to the evacuation centre. That way. This street's not safe.'

'Doctors,' Ben said briefly. 'We need to be at the hospital.'

And all of a sudden they had a military escort and Ben held her hand tighter and it seemed even more...right that she held his. And held and held.

It was so silent, so dark—and then they rounded the bend and the hospital was in front of them and it wasn't dark at all.

Kaimotu Hospital was a small weatherboard hospital up on the headland, looking over the town. Once it had been a gracious old house overlooking the harbour. Over the years it had been extended, with a brand-new clinic at the rear, a doctor's apartment to the side, the rooms expanded to make a lovely ten-bed hospital with most rooms looking out over the veranda to the harbour beyond.

It had been expanded even more now. Some sort of camp hospital had been set up on the front lawns overlooking the sea. It was a vast canvas canopy, lit by floodlights on the outside and by vast battery-powered lanterns inside. A huge red generator was humming from the side of the tent, and the lights were on inside the hospital.

Ginny, who'd thought bleakly of dealing with casualties in third world conditions, felt herself relax. Just a little.

'Docs,' the soldier escorting them said briefly, as yet another soldier came forward to greet them. 'Two of 'em. You can use them?'

'Doctors?' A fresh-faced kid who looked about eighteen pushed aside the canvas door and looked at them. 'Real doctors?'

'Ben McMahon and Ginny Koestrel,' Ben said, and held his hand out in greeting. 'I'm a family doctor with surgical training and Ginny's an anaesthetist.'

'Whew.' The guy whistled. 'I'm Dave Marr, doc with New Zealand Search and Rescue. We have Lou Blewit here as well but I want to send her back with the next chopper. I have a guy with a crush injury to his chest—breathing compromised. He needs a thoracic surgeon. If you guys can help…'

He was dressed in green theatre garb. He might look young but he didn't sound young, Ginny thought. He sounded every inch a doctor, like he knew exactly what he was doing.

Thank God for emergency personnel. Thank God for helicopters. If she and Ben had been on their own…

'You guys swear you're doctors?' Dave said, his tired face breaking into a slight smile. 'You look like chimney sweeps to me. Was that what kept you?'

'Digging the odd person out,' Ben said. 'We got here as fast as we could.'

'Well, thank God for it,' Dave said bluntly. 'From now on...yeah, we need diggers but we need doctors more. I have a truckload of casualties coming in now. You ready to deal with them?'

'Yes,' they said in unison, and Dave grinned.

'Excellent. You guys use the theatre inside the hospital—that's what you're familiar with. I'll stay on triage out here—this is my territory. By the way, you might need to wash. We've set up a washroom over there—we've attached hoses to the garden tanks out back but use a bit more antiseptic than usual because Abby tells us the tank often holds the odd dead possum. We're working on a safe water supply now.'

He glanced up as a battered farm truck turned into the car park. 'Here's the next load,' he said. 'Let's go.'

For the next eight hours Ginny and Ben scarcely had time to breathe.

Luckily most of the injuries were minor, caused by flying debris and masonry. The most common presentation was lacerations. Most of the island homes were weather-board with corrugated-iron roofs. If they'd been brick homes with slate or tile roofs, the injuries would have been more severe, but corrugated iron, crashing down in sheets, could slice to the bone. Added to that, people had crawled out of collapsed buildings, trying to get out as fast as they could, often unaware that they had been crawling over shattered glass and crockery.

The wounds were caked with dust, and they couldn't be stitched fast.

Some people needed to be transferred to the mainland. Some would need plastic surgery to stop scarring for a life-time, but there was enough work to hold Ben and Ginny in Theatre, working as hard and fast as they could.

They worked side by side rather than together, seeing two

patients at a time. They shared a nurse—Prue, the youngest of the island's nurses—and they helped each other.

It was hardly best medical practice to operate on two patients in the one small theatre but it meant help was always on hand. If one of them got into trouble, Ben helped Ginny or Ginny helped Ben. Ben's surgical skills assisted Ginny, Ginny's anaesthetic skills assisted Ben...

And besides...

It settled her, Ginny thought as she worked through the night. The day had been terrifying. Just the fact that she had Ben six feet away, a solid, reassuring presence, helped her to focus.

There was no question that she was a doctor now. She'd walked away from medicine six months ago but now she was in medicine up to her neck.

And for the first time in years she felt grateful to be a doctor.

She'd helped Ben save Henry but she'd been almost resentful that she'd been hauled out of her reclusive shell. Here there was no resentment.

She liked being able to help. She loved having the necessary skills.

The knowledge was almost like a lightning bolt. She remembered the early days of training, working as an intern. She remembered the almost terrifying sensation of making a difference to people's lives. The dependence on colleagues. The gut-wrenching pain of loss and the mind-blowing feeling of success. She remembered heading to the pub after work with a group of colleagues to unwind, joking about the macabre, understanding each other, knowing she'd be working side by side with them the next day.

Like she was working side by side with Ben now.

It had all stopped when she'd met James. Her social life

had centred on him from that point on. She'd started specialist anaesthetic training.

She'd still worked in a team in Theatre but the atmosphere had subtly changed. She had become the girlfriend of a senior consultant and James had often stopped by, to watch, to give a little advice, to make sure everyone in the theatre knew she was his woman.

Why was she thinking of that now? She was cleaning slivers of glass from Bea Higgins's knees. Bea was seven years old, she'd been having a day off school when the quake had hit because she'd needed to go to the dentist, and had ended up crawling out of the Higgins's lean-to bathroom.

'And Mum says I still have to go to the dentist,' she said mournfully.

'Cheer up,' Ben said from the other side of the room. He was stitching an elderly farmer's arm—Craig Robb had been trying to get his pigs out of their sty when sheets of corrugated iron had fallen and slashed. Farmer, not pig. 'Doc Dunstan's front porch has collapsed,' he told Bea. 'You might not get a dentist appointment for months.'

'Cool.' Bea grinned happily as Ginny dressed her cuts and grazes. She'd hurt when the anaesthetic wore off, Ginny thought, but kids bounced back. For most of these kids this earthquake would end up being an adventure.

And for the rest of the island? The damage didn't seem massive. There'd been no tsunami. There hadn't been any reports of multiple deaths—three so far, and all of them elderly. Could the island get off so lightly?

But there might well be more casualties. There were still the islanders who lived in outlying areas, where searchers hadn't been able to reach. There was still a trapped school bus.

There was still Henry.

'Worry about what's in front of you right now,' Ben said.

She flashed a glance at him and thought again, He knows me as no one else does.

The thought was terrifying, yet she was suddenly no longer terrified. She was working side by side with him, and no matter what was happening in the outside world, she wasn't terrified at all.

All his attention should be on his island. All his focus should be on deaths, injuries, damage.

Instead, he was working alongside Ginny Koestrel and it felt…okay.

As a seventeen-year-old he'd thought he loved her. Love was a pretty big word—a word he reserved for his family. There'd been a few women since Ginny, but not one he'd applied the 'love' word to.

His mother had been suggesting he could get together with Abby. Abby was competent, a caring professional, pretty, smiley, a great mum to her little boy. 'Does the fact that she has a child stop you being interested?' his mother had asked him recently, and he'd laughed. It made not one whit of difference. He'd lived in a household of twelve kids. If he didn't like kids he'd have gone nuts long since.

So what had been stopping him? He and Abby had dated a couple of times—yeah, okay, just social functions like the hospital fundraiser where it was easier to have a partner—but they had still been dates.

There'd been friendship and laughter, but not a single spark.

And here was this woman, this stranger, really, as he hadn't seen her for twelve years, working alongside him. She was a different person from the one he'd thought he'd been in love with all those years ago, yet sparks were flying everywhere.

How could there be sparks when he was so tired?

How could he hear her talk softly to Bea and crane his neck to hear, just to listen to her voice?

How could he get close? How could he brush away all the wounds that had been inflicted on her—for he knew there were deep wounds. How could he help her move on?

Move on towards him?

They ushered Craig and Bea out at the same time. Their two patients were welcomed into the arms of their relieved relatives, and there was a moment's peace while they waited for Dave to direct them to the next need. The young nurse, Prue, was almost dead on her feet. 'Go home,' Ben told her. 'You've done brilliantly.'

She left and Ben put his arms around Ginny and held her.

'So have you,' he said.

They stood at the entrance to the makeshift emergency hospital, and for a moment all was silent.

He kissed her lightly on her hair. 'You're doing a fantastic job, Dr Koestrel,' he told her. 'As a medical team, we rock.'

She didn't pull back. She was exhausted, she told herself as he tugged her closer. It was okay to lean on him.

The queue outside had disappeared. Islanders were settling into the refuge centre or in some cases stubbornly returning to their homes. There'd still be myriad minor injuries to treat, she thought, but Dave hadn't been waiting for them when they'd emerged this time.

There was this moment to stand in this man's arms and just…be.

It couldn't last. Of course it couldn't. A truck arrived and a weary-looking Dave emerged from the back.

'I need you to see two more patients and then I'm standing us all down,' he said. 'I'm dealing with a suspected early labour—I'll stay with her until the team arrives to evacuate her. I think she'll settle but I'm taking no chances.'

'Who?' Ben asked.

'A tourist,' Dave told her. 'She was on a boat in the harbour when it hit.' He grinned. 'Which is something of a relief because the islanders want Ben first, Ginny as second best and me a poor last. But, as I said, it's easing. We have paramedics who'll stay on call for the rest of the night and I have another doctor flying in to take over from me. It's four now. If anything dire happens we'll call you out but you need to catch some sleep. The searchers will find more at first light so medically things will speed up again. Is there anywhere here you both can sleep?'

'My apartment's at the back of the hospital,' Ben said. 'If it's anything like the rest of the hospital it'll be unscathed. Ginny can stay with me.'

'I can give you a bed in a tent if that's not okay,' Dave told her, but Ginny shook her head, even though the tent might be more sensible.

But she didn't feel sensible. She was still leaning against Ben. She still wanted to lean against him.

But there were problems. She needed to focus on something other than this man's arms.

'Button...' she started.

'Whoops, I have a message about someone called Button,' Dave told her, looking rueful. 'One of the guys passed it on. The message is that Ailsa and Hannah said to tell you that Button and Shuffles are fast asleep and happy. They also said to tell you someone's left a basket of kittens with Ailsa because their laundry's collapsed and apparently Ailsa is a sucker for animals, so the message continues that Ailsa says Button would like a black one with a white nose. Button says she wants to call it Button, too.'

He grinned, pleased with himself for remembering the full gist of the message, and Ginny found herself smiling, too. It was exactly the kind of message she needed to hear.

She found herself sniffing and when Ben's arm tightened around her she didn't resist. How could she pull away?

Weirdly, her world, which had been shaken to the core years before, the day James had got his diagnosis, or even earlier, she thought, maybe even the day her father and James had taken her to dinner and hammered into her that she was a fool not to specialise, a fool to keep working in the emergency medicine she loved, seemed, on this day of all days, to be settling.

'You said...' she managed. 'You said...we have two more patients to see?'

'Minor problems,' Dave said. 'The searchers have just swept the wharf. Brian Grubb was trapped in the co-op storeroom when the door shifted on its hinges. He's cut his leg and needs an X-ray to eliminate a fracture to his ankle.

'We also have a Mr Squid Davies—a venerable old gentleman. The search dogs found him under a pile of cray pots and they've brought him in, protesting. He's had a bang on his head. I can't see any sign of concussion but he didn't have the strength to heave the pots off himself. He tells us he forecast the earthquake. He's busy telling all and sundry, "I told you so." Are you sure you can handle it?'

Squid and his end-of-the-world forecasting. Could she handle it?

She grinned at Ben and he grinned back.

'It'll be a pleasure to treat him,' Ben said, and his smile warmed places inside her she hadn't even known had been cold. 'We might even concede we should have listened.'

CHAPTER SEVEN

BEN TOOK ON Brian; Ginny took on Squid. Squid was brought in on a stretcher, but he was sitting bolt upright, his skinny legs dangling down on either side.

'I can walk, you fellas,' he was protesting. 'One hit on the head and you think you can treat me like a namby-pamby weakling.'

'Indulge us,' Ginny said, as the hefty paramedics transferred him smoothly to her examination couch. 'Come on, Mr Davies, lie down and let me see that bump on your head.'

'Since when have I been Mr Davies?' Squid demanded. 'I'm Squid. And you're the Koestrel girl. Bloody uppity parents. Folks say you turned out all right, though.'

'I think she's all right,' Ben said from the other side of the theatre. 'What about you guys?' he asked the paramedics. 'Do you think she's all right?'

There were grunts of agreement from the two burly paramedics, from Brian and from Squid himself, and Ginny thought, wow, she'd been in an earthquake, she'd spent half a day digging people out from under rubble, she'd been working as an emergency doctor for hours...and they thought...

'She's cute,' Squid decreed.

'Nah,' one of the paramedics said, eying her red hair with appreciation. 'It's politically incorrect to say cute. How about handsome? Handsome and flaming?'

'You've got rocks in your head, all of you,' Ginny said, as Ben chuckled. It was four in the morning. She felt punch-drunk. They all must be punch-drunk. 'Speaking of heads, lie down, Squid, while I check yours.'

'Won't,' said Squid.

'Lie down or I take over,' Ben growled, 'and we'll do the examination the hard way.'

'You and whose army?'

'Do you know how many soldiers we have outside? Lie down or we'll find a fat one to sit on you. Now.'

And there was enough seriousness in his tone to make Squid lie down.

Someone—Margy? —had been organised enough to find the islanders' health files and set them at hand. Ginny could see at a glance if there were any pre-conditions that could cause problems. She flicked through Squid's file fast while Ben started work on Brian. Ben knew each patient inside out; he didn't need their histories, but Ginny was wise enough to take care.

She flipped through Squid's history and did a double-take at his age. Ninety-seven.

Prostate cancer. Treatment refused. Check-ups every six months or so, mostly *or so*, because *regular* didn't seem to be in Squid's dictionary.

A major coronary event ten years ago.

Stents and bypass refused.

'There's nothing wrong with me but a bump on the head,' Squid said sourly. 'There I was, minding me own business, when, *whump*, every cray pot in the shed was on top of me. I warned 'em. Don't you stack 'em up there, I said, 'cos the big one's coming. Didn't I say the big one was coming, Doc?'

'You did,' Ben said wryly. 'I would have thought, though, with your premonition, you would have cleared out of the way of the cray pots.'

'I'm good but I'm not that good,' Squid retorted. He'd submitted as Ginny had injected local anaesthetic around the oozing gash across his forehead but he obviously wasn't worrying about his head. 'I was right, though. Wasn't I right, Doc? That German doc was right, too, heading for home. But you stayed here. And you, too, miss,' he said to Ginny. 'Did you listen? No.'

'Yeah, but I didn't get hit on the head with cray pots,' Ginny retorted. 'So I must have done something sensible. Squid, you have fish scales in this wound!'

'I was wearing me hat. There's always fish scales in that hat. Dunno where it is now; expect I'll have to go digging for it. Get 'em out for me, there's a lass, and make it neat. I don't want to lose me handsome exterior. Not but what I'm getting past it for the need for handsome,' he added, swivelling on the table to look thoughtfully at Ben. 'Not like you two. Not past it at all, not you two. At it like rabbits you were when you were kids. Going to take it up again now?'

'We were not,' Ginny retorted, 'at it like rabbits.' This night was spinning out of control. She was close to exhaustion, but also close to laughter. *At it like rabbits?*

'You woulda been if that gimlet-eyed mother of yours would have let you,' Squid retorted. 'But now you can. Got a littlie, now, though. Does that make a difference, Doc?' he demanded of Ben.

'That is not,' Ben said levelly, 'any of your business.'

'Island business is my business,' Squid said happily. The local anaesthetic was taking hold and any pain that might have interfered with his glorious I-told-you-so attitude was fading fast. 'That's why I warned you. The big 'un's coming. Did you listen? Not you. People are dead, Doc, 'cos they didn't listen.' He lay back, crossed his arms and his smile spread beatifically across his ancient face. 'Told you so. Told you so, told you so, told you so.'

'Ginny, could you give me a hand with Brian's X-ray?' Ben said, grinning across at Squid's obvious bliss. 'It'll take a couple of moments for that anaesthetic to work, and I'd rather not call any of the nurses back. Squid, I want you to lie still and keep quiet. We have patients resting just through the canvas.' Then, as Squid opened his mouth to protest, he put up a hand in a peremptory signal for him to stop.

'Squid,' he said sternly. 'Rest on your laurels. You said the big one was coming and it did. The whole island's in awe. Enough. Lie there and think about it, but while you're thinking, stay still. We're taking Brian next door for an X-ray and when we get back I don't want you to have moved an inch. Right?'

'R-right,' Squid said in a voice that told Ginny he wasn't quite as brave as he was pretending to be. He really was a very old man. He would have been scared.

She put a hand on his shoulder and gave it a gentle squeeze. 'This'll take no more than five minutes,' she told him. She'd checked his vital signs. She'd checked his pupils, his reactions. His bump on the head seemed to be just that, a bump on the head. 'You won't move, will you?'

'Not if you promise to keep looking after me,' Squid said, recovering, and Ginny smiled.

'I promise.'

'Then off you go, Brian, and let the lady photograph you,' Squid decreed. 'She's some lady, isn't she, Doc?

'I… Yes,' Ben said.

'Good call,' Squid said. 'I think I'm about to make another prediction. You want to hear it?'

'No,' Ginny and Ben said together, too fast, and they wheeled Brian out of the door towards X-Ray before Squid could say another word.

* * *

The X-ray took effort on both their parts. They were both needed to do the roll transfer that was part of their training. From there the X-ray went smoothly, confirming a greenstick fracture.

'I'll put a simple splint on it tonight,' Ben told Brian. 'We'll check it again tomorrow—it'll need a full cast but we'll wait until the swelling goes down.'

'Good luck,' Ginny said. Because she was feeling more and more like an islander, she gave the burly farmer a hug, then headed back to attend to Squid.

He was curled on his side, his back to the door.

'Sorry I've been so long,' she said cheerfully, and crossed the six steps to the examination couch.

But by the third step she knew something was amiss. Dreadfully amiss.

The stillness was wrong. She'd seen this.

Breathing was sometimes imperceptible but when it wasn't present, you knew.

She knew.

'Ben,' she called, in the tone she'd been taught long ago as a medical student. It was a tone that said, I don't intend to frighten any other patient but I want you here fast. Now.

She put a hand on Squid's leathery neck as she called, her fingers desperately searching for a pulse.

There wasn't one.

Ben was with her almost instantaneously, the door closed firmly between them and Brian.

They were alone in the room. Ben and Ginny and Squid.

Or Ben and Ginny.

'Oh, God, I shouldn't have left him.' Ginny was hauling the equipment trolley from the side of the room, fumbling for patches. No pulse... She didn't even have monitors set up. No IV lines. She hauled Squid's shirt open, ripping buttons.

She was barely aware that Ben was with her. Where was the laryngosope? She needed an endotracheal tube.

Panic was receding as technical need took over, and the knowledge that everything she needed was in reach. She put the patches on with lightning speed...

And Ben grabbed her hands.

'No,' he said.

What the...? She hauled back, confused. They had so little time before brain damage was irreversible. Did he want monitors? Proof? 'Ben, there's nothing—'

'Exactly,' he said, and his hands held hers in a grip that brooked no opposition. 'And that's the way he'd want it.'

'What do you mean? He's healthy. He was sitting up. It's only a bump on the head. Let me go!'

'No,' he said. 'Leave it.' And he held her for longer, while Squid's body settled more firmly into that awful stillness, while the time for recovery, for miracles, passed them by.

'Let me go.' She could hardly make herself coherent. 'Are you mad?'

'I'm not mad. Squid's ninety-seven, Ginny,' Ben said, and his voice was implacable. 'He's left clear instructions. You think he'd thank us for trying to resuscitate him?'

'He's well. It's just the shock.' She was still struggling but it was already too late. There'd been such a tiny window of opportunity. That Ben could stand there and stop her... That Ben could do nothing...

'He's your friend,' she hurled at him, and it was an accusation.

It was also true.

True for her as well?

When they'd been kids Squid had taught them to fish for flounder, to jag for the squid he'd taken his name from. He'd also shared the eternal supply of aniseed balls he'd always carried in his back pocket.

He was almost a part of the island itself. For Ginny... The thought that this was the end...

She gave one last despairing wrench and finally Ben set her free. But even as he did so, she knew it was too late. She knew it. She felt cold fury wash through her that she hadn't been allowed to fight. She wanted to hit out, hit something. Hit Ben?

'You know about medical DNRs,' Ben said, watching her, calmly questioning. Do Not Resuscitate. 'Squid signed one years ago.'

'But they're for people who have no chance,' she managed, thinking of a counsellor handing a form to James, 'Do Not Resuscitate', and James screwing it into a ball and hurling it back.

'That's for people whose life is worthless. I don't need it, dammit.'

Her father had acted the same way. He'd had three coronary occlusions, a cardiac arrest, pacemaker fitted, defibrillator, there was nothing more to be done, yet he'd never have dreamed of signing a form that said 'Do Not Resuscitate'.

'Do not go gently into that good night.' Dylan Thomas's words had been her father and James's mantra, drilled into her with fury.

That anger was with her now. Not to be permitted to fight...

This was why she'd walked away from medicine, because she couldn't win. Because she wasn't good enough to win. To make a conscious decision not to win seemed appalling.

'Ginny, Squid is ninety-seven years old,' Ben said again, placing strong hands on her rigid shoulders. He must feel her anger but he was overriding it. 'He might look as if he's weathered to age for ever, but he's been failing for a long time. He has arthritis in almost every joint. He can't do the fishing he loves, and he's been getting closer and closer to needing nursing-home care. Add to that, from the moment the earth shook his face has been one vast smile. He was right, we were wrong. You don't think that's a good note to go out on?'

But how could death be a good note? 'We could have…'

'We could have for what, Ginny?' Ben said, still in that gentle yet forceful voice that said he saw things behind her distress and her anger. Things she didn't necessarily want him to see.

'You have to fight.' She could hardly speak. So many emotions were crowding in. James's words, flooding back…

You stupid cow, get the medication right, you know I need more. Damn what the oncologist says, give me more now!

'No,' Ben was saying. 'If we pulled Squid back now, what then? You know cardiac arrest knocks blood flow to the brain. You know the really old struggle to re-establish neural pathways. Ginny, he's left us at the moment of his greatest triumph and I for one wouldn't ask for anything better for such a grand old man.'

Anger was through and through her, but behind it was a fatigue that was almost overwhelming. It was like all the emotions that had built within her from the moment of James's death were here in this room, the armour she'd tried to place around herself shattering into a thousand pieces.

'I fight the battles I want to win,' Ben said. 'I wouldn't want to win this one.'

'You didn't want him to live?'

'I want everyone to live,' he said evenly, refusing to rise to the emotion she was hurling at him. 'But at ninety-seven I know where to stop. Ginny…'

'Don't Ginny me,' she whispered, and he touched her

face, to give pause to the hysteria she was so close to. She flinched and he stopped dead.

'Is that what happened?' he said. 'Did James hit you because you couldn't save his life?'

There was a moment's deathly silence. Okay, more than a moment, Ginny conceded. There was a whole string of moments, packed together, one after the other, leading to a place where she was terrified to go.

'No,' she said finally in a dead, cold voice, a voice she scarcely recognised as her own. She glanced at Squid, at the peace on the old man's face, and she knew Ben was right. She knew it. She had no reason to be angry with him.

There was a time to die and that Squid had died at his moment of greatest triumph... *A consummation devoutly to be wished?*

Maybe, but that was the problem, she thought. James and her father had seen death as defeat. It was why, afterwards, she'd walked away from medicine. To see death, time and time again...

'No,' she said, and then decided it was time to be honest. 'Okay, once. Towards the end. Don't think of me as a battered wife, though, Ben. I was no doormat. Yes, I put up with abuse when he was dying, but he was dying. The one time he slapped me I walked away for a week. Then I had a call from the hospital saying he'd had a bleed. I had no choice but to go back. James lashed out because I was living and he wasn't. There was nothing I could do but put up with it until it was done.'

He did touch her then, a feather touch on her cheek. 'You should never have put up with it. Dying gives no one the right to abuse another. That someone could hit you...'

'It's okay.'

'It's never okay.'

'Yet you say Squid's death is okay.'

'You equate death with violence? It's not the same thing, Ginny, and you know it. Not a peaceful, timely death at the end of a life well lived.'

There was another of those silences. The searchers had ceased for the night, ready to start again at daybreak. The stream of incoming patients had ended.

'Is this why you took Button?' Ben asked finally, heavily. 'Because you felt obligated? Like you felt obligated to return to James?'

'No.' She shook her head fiercely at that. 'No way. Do you really think of me as a wimp?'

'No, but—'

'I did go back to James because he was dying and there was no one else to care,' she said. 'But Button's no obligation. The way I see it, Button's the one true thing that's come out of this. Veronica and James can betray all they like, but to hurt Button... I'll love her and we'll make a new life for ourselves, without their shadows.'

'Good for you,' Ben said, a trifle unsteadily, and then he touched her face again. 'And this time you didn't even flinch. You're some woman, Ginny Koestrel.' He hesitated, glancing down at Squid.

'I'll organise this,' he told her. There'd be paperwork, formalities for Squid that had to be done and they had to be done now. Medical imperatives had to take over. 'You fix Brian's splint and then we need bed. We're both exhausted. Too much emotion. Too much work. Too much...everything.' His hands were on her shoulders again, but there was no force, only warmth and reassurance and friendship.

And something more?

'I...I do need to find Button,' she managed.

'Mum and Hanna have Button safe. They won't thank you for waking them, and you know they'll contact you in a heartbeat if Button needs you. My apartment's here. Stop fighting the world, Ginny. Squid's stopped fighting. It's time you stopped, too.'

It was four-thirty when Ben finally led Ginny into his apartment at the rear of the hospital. She was so tired she could barely stand. She should sleep in the search and rescue tents, she thought, or in the refuge centre or...or...

Or stop fighting. Stop thinking she had to fight.

'Bed,' Ben said. 'The bathroom's through that door. You want pyjamas, there're spares in the bureau, bottom drawer. They'll be big on you but they'll be comfy. There's a spare toothbrush in the bathroom cabinet.'

'You're ready for anything,' she murmured.

'I'm ready for any of my eleven siblings to land on my doorstep any time,' he said dryly. 'You try having brothers and sisters on an island as small as Kaimotu. *Ben, Mum'll have a fit if she sees me like this. Ben, I just need a bit of quiet. Ben, no one at home understands me.* This place doubles as the McMahon refuge centre.'

'You have lucky brothers and sisters,' she said wearily, and looked at the nice, big sofa in the sitting room. 'This'll do me nicely, as I suspect it does your siblings. Thank you, Ben. Goodnight.'

'You're using the bed.'

'I'm not taking your bed. There's no need. The way I feel, I'd sleep on stones.'

'Me, too,' he said, and then there was silence. A long silence.

Exhausted or not, things were changing. Twisting. It was like a void was opening, a siren was calling them in.

'I don't suppose,' Ben said, oh, so casually, 'that you'd like to share.'

'Ben...'

'No, okay, not an option,' he said hastily. 'I'd never sleep with a woman who expects a raised hand to be followed by a slap.'

'I know it wouldn't,' she said, astounded. 'I know it never would be.'

'And I'd never sleep with a woman who thought I might blame her for things that go wrong.'

That was a bigger statement. It was a statement to take her breath away.

Not all men were like James or like her father, the statement said.

Ben was her friend.

But Ben was standing in front of her now and she knew he was asking to be much more.

Sharing a bed...

More even than that.

'We do need to sleep,' she said uncertainly, but *more* was right in front of her, a huge, overwhelming impossibility that suddenly seemed possible.

To take a moment that had happened all those years ago— and take it forward?

Ben's hands were on her shoulders again—she was starting to get used to it. She was starting to get used to the feel of him. To the comfort of him. To security and to caring.

To love?

How could she possibly think that? How could she possibly fall in love again?

But right now fatigue was taking the edges off fear and caution and the knowledge that love could haul your life out of control and spin it into a crazy vortex of darkness. Right now there was only Ben, gently propelling her into his bedroom.

He proposed to sleep out here. Alone. Well, why not? He'd

asked to share and she'd reacted with fear. The moment she had, he'd backed away.

He'd never push. He respected her.

Did she want respect?

The feel of his hands…

The knowledge that his body was right here, right now…

The fact that this was Ben…

Things were twisting, changing. She was feeling like a caterpillar cocooned in her impenetrable skin, only suddenly the skin was bursting.

She wasn't sure what was inside.

She wasn't sure, but Ben was here, now. Her lovely Ben.

No matter what this night had held, no matter about her armour, no matter about all her vows, this man was a huge imperative overriding all else.

Instead of allowing him to twist her away, to propel her away, she twisted back, so she stood within his hold, so close she could feel his breath, so close she could feel his heartbeat.

'Ben,' she said, and she looked up at him and he looked down at her and she knew she didn't have to say a word. Everything that had to be said had been said.

'You know I love you,' he said, and the world held its breath.

Love?

'I always have,' he said conversationally. 'I may not always have been faithful…'

'Not? When I'd imagined you pining for years and years?' Somehow she managed to sound shocked, and somehow, amazingly, there was laughter in the room.

'No, but when you smacked Robbie Cartwright over the head with a wet chaff bag because he'd spilled my tadpoles and then went down on your hands and knees and scoured the mud until every last tadpole was saved…I fell in love with you then. Yes, Ginny Koestrel, there have been other women, as there have been other men for you, but our love was forged when we were eight years old and it seems it's there for life.'

'Ben...'

'And I'm not teasing,' he said softly, laughter fading. 'I have no idea why this emotion has surfaced again after all these years but it has, and if you'd care to share my bed...'

'But in the morning...'

'Can we worry about the morning in the morning?' he asked. 'Ginny, this is just for here, for now. It's been one hell of a day. Say no now and we'll sleep apart, but...'

'Yes,' she said. 'I'm saying yes.'

There was a moment's loaded pause. Maybe more than a moment. She looked up at him and he was so...solid. Here.

This man had been her friend for life. She'd walked away from him for all sorts of reasons, some of them right, some of them wrong, but now, for this night, he was offering her love and warmth and desire.

Love...

This wasn't a going-down-on-bended-knee love, she thought. This was a love born of friendship. She knew, she just knew, that taking what Ben was offering would never be used to hurt her, to hold her, to commit.

He wanted her in his bed now, in his arms, and there was no place she'd rather be.

'It's nearly five,' she whispered. 'We need to sleep.'

'So we do,' he said.

'So you'd best make love to me now,' she said, 'because there's no way I can sleep without it—except with drugs, and I don't hold with drugs when there's a very sensible alternative.'

'Is that what I am?' Amazingly laughter was suddenly all around them. 'A sensible alternative?'

'Yes,' she said, and she lifted her arms and wound them

around his neck and then she raised her face to be kissed. 'My Ben,' she said. 'My prescription tranquilliser.'

'If you think I'm your tranquilliser,' Ben said, sweeping her into his arms and carrying her toward the bed, without so much as a hint of asking permission, 'then you have another think coming. Tranquilliser indeed. Is that what you really need, Dr Koestrel? Something to make you sleep?'

'N-no,' she managed.

'Excellent.' He lowered her onto the soft covers of his big, masculine bed and hauled his shirt over his head.

She'd seen this man's body—in swimming trunks, when he'd been seventeen.

She hadn't seen this. His body...his big, lovely body. It took her breath away.

'Ben...'

He stopped, the laughter disappearing again.

'Ginny?' His voice was tender and she knew if she said stop now, no would mean no.

Where did friendship end and love take over?

Right here, she thought. Right now.

'Come here,' she whispered, and she tugged him down to join her. 'You've done enough. The least I can do is help you get that belt unbuckled.'

He laughed and submitted. He was undoing the buttons of her blouse. It was already ripped. She should tell him to rip it straight off but he was over her, half straddling her, concentrating on each button, and her mind was doing some sort of weird shutting-down thing.

Only it wasn't shutting down. It was sort of...focussing. Every single distraction was disappearing to nothing. Earthquakes. Button. Patients. The past and the future. Nothing mattered. There was only this man carefully, painstakingly undoing buttons on a ruined blouse.

She put her fingers up and ran her palms down the length

of his chest to where his belt was unfastened. She could go lower but Ben was taking his time and so was she.

The buttons were no longer an issue. He spread her shirt wide. 'You want me to tug it free?' he asked, and she grabbed both sides of the skimpy fabric and ripped.

'Wow,' Ben said. 'You want to do that to your bra as well?'

'You have to work for it,' she said, smiling and smiling, and he did, and then a few very satisfactory moments followed while he explored what was underneath.

She was on fire. It didn't actually matter if this night wasn't consummated, she thought hazily, but then his fingers drifted further, and she forgot any thoughts of lack of consummation. Consummation did matter. She wanted him. This was here, this was now. This was Ben.

And as a faint aftershock rippled across the island, waking weary rescue workers and causing islanders to hold each other tighter, Dr Ben McMahon and Dr Guinevere Koestrel didn't notice.

In a few short hours they'd be back in the wards, back to being emergency doctors.

For now there was only this night, this heat, this need.

For now there was only each other.

CHAPTER EIGHT

SHE DIDN'T WANT dawn to come. She lay encircled in Ben's arms and she thought if she didn't move maybe time would stand still. She was spooned against Ben's body, skin to skin, warm, protected…loved?

Somewhere out there was the outside world, responsibilities, cares, life, but for Ginny right now life was solely within this man's arms, and she wanted nothing more.

He was awake. She felt him shift slightly and the tingle of naked skin was enough to make her tremble. He kissed her hair and then tugged her around so she was facing him and he could kiss her properly. Deeply, achingly wonderful.

And then, as she knew he must, he set her back, holding her at arm's length, and they both knew the world needed to intrude.

'We've had four hours' sleep,' he said ruefully.

'Three and a half,' she said, and smiled, and he kissed her again.

'I know,' he said, half-mournfully. 'A man had the promise of four hours' precious sleep and suddenly there was a seductress in my bed.'

'You didn't appear,' she said smugly, 'to take very much seducing.'

'We need to go, Ginny.'

'We do.' She needed to find Hannah and check on Button, before heading back to the hospital. With the dawn the searchers would be out again and there'd be another influx of injured islanders.

Please, let the worst of it be past, she pleaded silently, and Ben kissed her again, but lightly this time, on the lips, and it was a kiss of reassurance.

'We can cope,' he said. 'Whatever the day brings, we'll face it. Ginny, will you share my bed again tonight?'

That was one to take her breath away.

'Ben...'

'I know it's too soon,' he told her. 'We're too stressed. This is hardly the time to be making a lifelong commitment and I'm not asking that. Okay, I'm not even asking for to-night, but if you're hanging around, wondering how to fill in time, and if the pillows up at the vineyard have dust on them, think of this as an alternative.' He touched her cheek, very gently, and his smile was a caress all by itself.

'Any time, my Ginny,' he said softly. 'This thing between us... I haven't figured it out and I know you're even fur-ther behind than I am, but I do know that I want you on my pillow, for tonight and for whenever you need me. I'll take my needs out of it for now because I know that they scare you. For now. I'm here, Ginny. I'll never hurt you and I'm just...here.'

For a while after that things got crazy. The two doctors with the rescue service plus every available nurse were fully in-volved caring for those who made their way to the extended hospital for treatment.

The main injury was lacerations, but there were broken bones, bruises that swelled into haematomas, twists, sprains and also fear. In some cases the fear was as much an injury as a bone break—a young mum who lived alone while her husband was away on a fishing trip was almost paralysed with terror and her terror was infecting her kids.

Medics turned into social workers, calling for help as they needed it. The young mum was matched with an elderly couple who had a lovely stable old weatherboard house that had remained unscathed. Their age meant they'd seen it all and they weren't the least bit bothered about what nature could throw at them, and they were warmly welcoming.

'Come and stay, as long as you like,' they told her when Ben contacted them and asked for their help, and Ginny watched Ben reassure everyone and she thought...

How could she ever have let herself believe family medicine was beneath her?

How could she ever have let James and her father persuade her?

Things still were changing inside her. They were twisting, jumbling, like the world had yesterday.

Last night had been world-changing for her. Today, working side by side with Ben, it changed even more.

She was so aware of him. She was so...

Discombobulated. It was the only word she could think of to describe how she felt. Weird, out of her body, where the only thing that kept her feet on the ground was seeing the next patient.

But finally they ran out of patients. By late morning the number of casualties was slowing to a trickle and she was able to surface and think of other imperatives.

She glanced around and thought, *I'm not needed here. Not for a while at least.*

'Ben, is it okay if I go and find Button?'

'Of course.' Hannah had popped in early to reassure Ginny that Button was fine but Ginny had been in mid-suture and hadn't been able to stop. 'I reckon she could do with a cuddle,' Ben told her.

'She's pretty good at giving them,' Ginny said, and Ben grinned.

'She is, that. So now you have two cuddlers. Off you go, Dr Koestrel, and find your alternative.'

And he kissed her, lightly, a feather kiss, but every eye in the big makeshift casualty ward was on them and she left with her face burning. She was feeling…feeling…

Even more discombobulated.

Practicalities. She needed to focus on what was necessary rather than what she was feeling, she told herself fiercely as she headed down from the hospital towards the town.

There were people everywhere. Even now, the chaos of last night was turning into organised chaos. Debris was being removed from the road, teams were going from house to house, inspecting damage, using paint to scrawl codes on each—'Safe', 'Safe With Care', 'Do Not Enter'.

And everywhere she went, people greeted her.

'Hey, Ginny, good to see you safe. You guys are doing a great job. So glad you're back. Great to have you here, lass, so glad you're home.'

This was….home. She knew it.

This morning she felt an islander. It was a strange sensation.

She'd never felt like she belonged, she thought. Had it taken an earthquake to make her put down roots?

And then she saw Hannah, heading up the road from Ailsa's house, carrying Button, and her stride quickened. Button. How fast had this little girl wrapped her way around her heart? She'd wanted so much to be with her last night. But then… But then…

To her dismay, she was blushing again, and she reached Hannah and took Button into her arms and buried her face in the softness of her new little daughter until the colour subsided.

As she knew she would, Button's arms wrapped around her in a bear hug.

'Ginny,' she said in satisfaction. 'Cuddle.'

It was the best thing. What was Veronica about, abandoning this little one? she thought. She'd lived with her for all of two weeks and already she was starting to think that if Veronica wanted her back she'd face a fight.

She needed to get those documents sorted. She needed to get the formal adoption through so that Veronica couldn't just swan in and take her away if the whim took her.

Ben would help.

All this she thought in the moments she took out to let her colour subside, to let the warmth of Button settle her, to feel even more that this was her home.

'How frantic are you?' Hannah asked when she finally emerged from her bear hug, and Ginny smiled ruefully.

'Sorry.' On impulse she hugged Hannah as well, with Button sandwiched between. 'I haven't even said thank you yet. Taking her in last night…'

'It was the least I could do, and I always do the least I can do,' Hannah said cheerfully. 'Mum and I had six toddlers between us. But no tragedies. They're all kids of those caught up in rescue efforts, like you and Ben.' Then her face clouded. 'But I heard Squid died.'

'Yes.' There was nothing else to say.

'Ben will be upset,' Hannah said quietly. 'He loved that old man.'

He didn't try to save him, Ginny thought, but she didn't say it. Ben's reasons were sound; she knew they were, but they took some getting her head around. She should have her head around it. Her reaction was illogical but it was still there.

You fought to the end, and if you failed…

Failure. It slammed back, right there and then, standing

on the rubble-strewn main street with Hannah watching her curiously and Button still clinging, nonjudgmental, her one true thing.

Was that why she loved her? Because Button would never judge her?

Would Ben ever judge her?

This was crazy. She gave herself a fierce mental shake and turned her attention back to the question Hannah had asked first.

How frantic are you?

'The worst of the rush is over,' she told her. 'We have four doctors, five nurses and for the time being not enough patients. Please, God, it stays that way.' She hesitated. 'I thought...if I could find a car... Henry's on his own out at his cottage behind the vineyard. I just met Ella—she's his closest neighbour but they were in town when the quake hit and haven't been back. Ella has a sprained wrist and is staying put. That means Henry's on his own. Ben and I drove down from the vineyard yesterday so I know a route we can take and we've already chopped the fences. I might just go and check.'

'Send a team,' Hannah said, and Ginny gazed along the street at the organised troops of orange-clad workers moving methodically from house to house.

'It's just one old man in a tiny weatherboard cottage,' she said. 'It's hardly worth a team and if I know Henry he'd be furious if I sent strangers.'

'So let him be furious.'

'No.' Ginny shrugged. She'd had enough blame in her life, she didn't need to wear this. 'It's easy enough to check and it's safe enough. I'll take one of the hospital vehicles.'

'You can take Mum's,' Hannah offered. 'It's four-wheel drive and it has a child seat.'

'Why—?'

'Um…that's why I was coming to find you,' Hannah said diffidently. 'There's been a bit of a drama with the school bus. Nothing dreadful,' she added as Ginny flinched. 'It was stuck between two landslips. They had a kid missing but they all seem to be accounted for now and as far as I know there's no casualties. But they're bringing them into town by boat now and lots of their mums and dads are still stranded in outlying parts of the island. So Mum and I have been asked to help. If you're sure where you're going is safe…could you take Button with you?'

She thought about it. The route she and Ben had taken yesterday had been bumpy but sound. They'd checked the farmhouses along the way so there'd be no huge dramas to find.

She could stop in at the vineyard, check the house was okay, maybe pick up a few things she would need if they were to stay in town. She'd take no risks.

And at Henry's cottage…

The worst she'd find would be an injured old man, but she was more likely to find him distressed than injured. And angry that she'd come?

Button could defuse that, she thought. She might even help.

'Take a radio with you,' Hannah urged. 'The rescue co-ordinator is giving them out. You'll need to tell him where you're going. Oh, and I'm off to let Ben know about the bus. He's been worried about Abby. I'll let him know where you've gone as well. Is that okay?'

She shouldn't take Button. She held her and thought there were risks. But the risks were small, and with no one to mind her… The alternative was to leave Henry without assistance he might need.

She could do this. It'd be safe.

'You do that,' she said, and gave Hannah another swift hug. 'And tell Ben I'll be fine. We'll all be fine. Let's hope we've heard the worst of the news about this earthquake. It's time to come out the other side.'

'She's gone where?'

'Up to Henry's.' Hannah suddenly sounded scared and Ben caught himself. He'd reacted with shock, and given a moment's thought he had himself together. The route they'd taken yesterday was safe enough. She had his mother's car, which was as tough as old boots. She was sensible.

'She took Button,' Hannah said, and he had to fight shock again.

But it was still reasonable. Woman heading off to check on an elderly neighbour, taking her daughter with her. Via a safe route. Taking a radio.

She was sensible and she'd be even more sensible with Button with her.

'Mum and I are heading down to the harbour to be there when the kids come in,' Hannah said. 'You want to come? Abby will be there.'

She was still matchmaking, Ben thought, humour surfacing. Ailsa and Hannah—plus half the island—had been trying to get Ben and Abby together for years.

It wasn't going to happen. They were friends but there'd never been that spark.

Like the spark of last night?

Last night hadn't been a spark, he conceded. It had been wildfire. A meeting of two bodies that ignited each other.

Ginny had ghosts.

He could lay ghosts to rest, though, he thought as Hannah waited for his reply. He could work with whatever demons she had; she lived here now and he had all the time in the world.

Except he wanted her in his bed again, tonight.

'It's Ginny, isn't it?' Hannah said cheekily.

And he wished he was busy. He needed a whole busload of casualties to come in the door this minute to stop the prying, laughing eyes of his little sister seeing far more than he wanted her to see.

'You're sure she's taken a radio?'

'Cross my heart and hope to break a leg. We walked to the co-ordination centre together. She's got more safeguards in place than you can shake a stick at. You know, Abby's been out all night with the most gorgeous rescue paramedic. You're not worried about Abby?'

'Not if she has the most gorgeous rescue paramedic with her.'

'But if it were Ginny?' Her eyes danced and she held up her hands. 'Okay, big brother, no more questions. I don't think I need to ask them anyway. I'm off to do some serious childminding.' She glanced around the makeshift casualty ward where medics were working efficiently and well. 'You know, if this place stays quiet you could even follow Ginny.'

'She doesn't need me.'

'She might,' Hannah said airily. 'You never know.'

It was kind of eerie retracing the route she and Ben had followed yesterday. Then their minds had been set to crisis mode. They'd faced fear and tragedy, and they'd known they had to get down to the hospital fast.

Now the crisis seemed to be over. It was a gorgeous autumn day. The rolling hills were bathed in warm sunshine, the cattle had gone back to grazing and only the occasional fallen tree or weird gash across a paddock indicated anything had happened.

The gashes were easy to avoid. They seemed to happen in fault lines, where the earth underneath had simply pulled apart. They didn't look deep but Ginny didn't need to find out how deep they were.

She could still see the tracks they'd made yesterday, driving the truck cross-country over the lush pastures. She kept to the tracks. She didn't deviate to the houses she passed—she knew they'd been checked. The fences were all slashed thanks to yesterday's efforts so she didn't need to stop until she reached the vineyard.

Her house was still intact.

She climbed from the car, lifted Button out and stood looking at it. The long, low homestead showed superficial damage—a couple of broken windows, downpipes skewed, the front steps to the veranda twisted away and one crumpled chimney—but nothing major.

The house had been shaken and then put down again on the same foundations and she stood and hugged Button and looked at it and felt her eyes well with tears.

Why? This had been her parents' holiday retreat. This place had only been home for her for six months.

But that's what it was. Home.

This island was home.

Ben was home?

She had a tiny flash of longing. She and Ben. Kids, dogs, family. Here?

Whoa, that was like a teenager sitting in class signing her name Ginny McMahon, over and over again. She'd actually done that when she was seventeen. Dumb. Emotional. Not based on facts.

But it might be, she thought. Last night had been real. Last night Ben had said he loved her.

So many emotions. She stood in the sun in the stableyard and for a moment she simply gave in to them. Yesterday the world had shaken, but for her, now, the world had settled, and her foundations seemed surer.

'This is home,' she whispered to Button. 'We'll fix this up. It's big and solid and safe. We can live here for ever and ever.'

And Ben? Big and solid and safe?

So sexy he made her toes curl?

That was way too much to think about right now. Ben and what had happened last night was an image, a presence, a sensation that had her retreating fast to the practical.

She and Button ventured round the back of the house to the kitchen. She turned on the hose—miraculously the water tanks were still standing and she still had pressure. Button's favourite occupation was still to stand and point the hose, and the late-producing tomatoes were wilting.

'Give them a big drink,' she told her, and knew she had a few minutes to enter the house. If she avoided standing under the beams she'd be safe enough. She needed to collect urgent belongings, things they'd needed to stay in the town for a few nights.

With Ben?

Don't go there. She was starting to feel…just a little bit foolish. More than a little bit afraid.

Get on with it. Move on, she told herself, and get back to the hospital. She might be needed. Coming up here was a bit irresponsible.

Unless Henry did need her.

She headed back out to the garage and grabbed bolt cutters for hacking through fences if needed, and then popped a happy, soggy Button back in the four-wheel drive. Henry's cottage was further out on the headland. The track seemed to be okay. There weren't any significant ruts or crevices, though at one place there was a small landslip partly blocking the way.

'Nothing to this, Button,' she told the little girl as they edged past. 'We'll reach Henry's cottage in no time. It'll be fine.'

And then they topped the next rise and saw the cottage and it wasn't fine at all.

Ben was starting to worry. It seemed simple, logical even, for Ginny to drive to Henry's. It didn't even seem risky to take Button with her. Childminders were at a premium, the way seemed safe and Ginny wasn't one to take risks.

So why was he worrying?

It wasn't as if he didn't have enough to do. The boatload of school kids had arrived, with myriad cuts and bruises to be checked. There was nothing serious but most of these kids had parents who'd spent a sleepless night imagining the worst, and every cut needed to be checked.

Besides, to a traumatised five-year-old a bandage was a badge of honour, a signal to the world that he'd been doing something dangerous. It was therapy all by itself, Ben thought as he applied a much-too-big plaster to Rowan March's grazed arm. He'd applied antiseptic with liberal abandon as well, so Rowan headed off with his parents, plus a bright orange arm and a plaster to brag about. He was all better. And suddenly there were no more kids.

'We have a bit of medical overkill.' Margy was clearing trays, keeping a weather eye on the door. 'So many helpers... The guys have been wonderful, though. Four deaths, five major injuries, minor injuries arriving slowly enough to be dealt with promptly, and teams are reporting most properties have been checked.'

'I should have sent a team out to Henry's,' Ben growled, and Margy frowned.

'Didn't Max and Ella check on him?'

'Apparently not. Their daughter's here in town. They came down in a rush and stayed.'

'I'll ask one of the rescue guys—'

'There's no need. Ginny's gone up there.'

'Has she now.' Margy eyed him thoughtfully. 'And that's why you seem distracted?'

'I'm not distracted.' Then he shrugged and grinned. 'Or not very.'

'You want to follow her up there?' Margy raised a quizzical eyebrow and smiled. What was it with the people around him? Was he that transparent? 'Surely she shouldn't be out there by herself.'

But one of the searchers was coming in now, cradling his arm. He needed to be seen to and the two fly-in doctors were taking a break. Margy and Ben were it.

'I don't have time.'

'But when the others come back on duty?'

'She'll be back by then.'

'So she will,' Margy said, pinning on a smile. 'So you can stop worrying.'

'I've got you worrying now,' he said.

'She's a sensible woman.' But Margy was starting to look worried.

'Will you cut it out? There's no reason to worry.'

'Except that if it was my Charlie I'd be worried,' Margy said. 'And the way you feel about Ginny...'

'What the...? I do not feel—'

'Sure you do,' she said, cheering up. 'You think you can sleep together on this island and not have every islander know in five minutes?'

'Margy! We were exhausted. She needed to stay in my apartment.'

'Of course,' Margy said equitably. 'But if you slept on the sofa I'm a monkey's uncle and if you're not feeling like I feel about Charlie, when you're looking the way you're looking...'

'Will you cut it out?'

'Yes, Doctor,' she said meekly. 'Anything you say, Doctor. But let's get this arm seen to and get you up the valley to rescue your lady.'

* * *

Henry's cottage was ramshackle. He'd run a small farm up here before her parents had employed him, but he'd let this place go. He'd only left the vineyard six months back, when arthritis had overtaken him, and he'd refused Ginny's offer to stay in the caretaker's residence permanently.

The old cottage, therefore, was hanging together with rotting timbers and rusty nails. Ginny had been out here a couple of times to see him. She'd been horrified but he wouldn't move.

And now…maybe the time for him to move was gone. The entire building had folded in on itself. The chimney looked as if it had crashed down, bringing the rest of the house with it.

It looked like a huge bonfire, set and ready to go.

And where was Henry?

'Stay in the car, Button,' Ginny said, handing Shuffles over. 'I need to see…'

'Henry,' Button said, and Ginny wondered how much this little girl understood. Henry had been down in the vineyard teaching Ginny to prune. He'd shown Button how to build Shuffles a little house with the clippings and then, the last time Ginny had come up here, the day after Henry came home from hospital, Henry had made Button red cordial, which she liked very much.

'I don't know where Henry is,' Ginny conceded. 'But you stay in the car while I look.'

'Okay,' Button said happily, and Ginny left the doors open so the sun wouldn't heat it up too much and turned her mind to Henry.

Somewhere in this mess, an old man…

The house was on the headland overlooking the sea. From here you could almost see to the mainland. A sea eagle was soaring in the thermals, seemingly having given up on fishing for the day just to soak up the sun. There seemed no urgency at all. How could anything dreadful happen on such a day?

Where was Henry?

'Henry?' It was a cautious call, and produced nothing. She tried again and put a bit of power behind it.

'Henry!'

And from the ruins...

'Well, about time. I've bin thinking I was going to have to chop me leg off with a penknife, only I can't reach a penknife. You want to get me out of here, Ginny, girl?'

Ginny, girl. He'd called her that all her life, she thought as she tried to get closer, tried to figure where exactly he was.

Feeling ill.

She should have insisted he stay with her. She thought suddenly that this man was more of a parent to her than her own parents were. Henry at the vineyard, Ailsa in town, her friend Ben—those were her people.

'Are you hurt?' she called, shifting to the far side of the house, calling loudly because he was far in, she could hear it from his voice.

'I'm stuck. Bloody piano came down on me ankle. I can still wiggle me toes. It got me sideways, like. I never even played the thing either. My May only got it 'cos she liked the look of it.'

He was sounding brave but she heard the pain and weakness behind the bravado. But how to get him out? She was looking at vast sheets of roofing iron topping a crumbling mess.

'I need to call for help,' she told him. 'Can you hold on for a bit?'

'Can you get me one of them intravenous line things you docs have? You could feed it down through the cracks with a bit of beer in it. A man 'd feel better with a beer in his belly.'

'You're still recovering from a stomach ulcer,' Ginny retorted. She had him pinpointed now, she thought. From the sound of his voice he was near the remains of the main chimney but completely under the roofing iron. 'No alcohol for you!'

'No, ma'am. But you're calling for help?'

'You'd better believe it.'

'Ben!'

Ben had just finished splinting the fractured arm. It was a vicious break; it'd need setting by a decent orthopaedic surgeon, but he'd done enough to make the guy comfortable. He was starting to clear up when Don Johnson, the island's fire chief, stuck his head around the door. 'Can I have a word?'

'Sure. You settle down on the pillows, Mac,' he told the guy he was treating. 'You'll be on the next chopper out of here.'

'Chopper'll be half an hour,' Don said across him, glancing at Mac with concern. 'Do you have decent painkillers on board, Mac? Can you wait until next trip?'

'Sure,' Mac said. 'Broken wing is all. I can still handle a shovel if you let me.'

'I don't need a shoveller,' Don said, but he sounded worried. 'What we need is more vehicles. Ben, Ginny's just contacted base. She's up on the headland past her place and Henry's trapped under his collapsed house. I'm hauling a team together now. Are you free as soon as we are?'

'I'm free now,' Ben said.

It was the longest wait. There was nothing she could do but sit in the sun by the ruin that was Henry's house, and cuddle Button and talk to him. If she tried to climb onto the ruin to rip up the sheets of iron that hid him from view, she could bring more down on the man beneath. She had to sit and wait, sit and wait, and Henry knew it.

'So tell me why you never came back?' Henry asked, and she shook herself and thought it was she who should be asking questions, she who should be focussing on keeping him distracted.

'I did come back.'

'From the time you were seventeen… Your parents came back every summer and played the landed gentry. Why not you?'

'I guess I didn't…like playing the landed gentry.'

'Or were you scared you'd fall harder for our Ben?' Henry said. 'That's what my May said. "She's fallen for that lad in a big way," she said. "If she comes back next summer they'll be together for life, mark my words," and then you never came back. So what was it about our Ben that scared you?'

'Nothing.' She was holding Button on her knee, making daisy chains to keep the little girl occupied. She was as close to Henry as she dared to go.

'Something did,' Henry said, and she heard the pain in his voice and knew he was trying hard to find anything—anything to distract him. 'You don't need to tell me, but May said you were as besotted with him as he was with you, and then you disappeared. It seemed dumb to us.'

'It was too hard,' she said, and she didn't say it loud enough. In truth it was barely a whisper.

'You still there?' Henry's voice rose sharply and she caught herself. This wasn't about her. This was about Henry and distraction and nothing else.

And maybe…maybe it was time to say it like it was.

'I wasn't brave enough to love him,' she said. 'I was seventeen and my parents treated this place as an escape. That summer…I told my mother I was in love with Ben, and she laughed. And then she told me exactly what would happen if…if I was stupid.'

'What would happen?'

His voice was so thin she was starting to panic. He sounded so weak there was no way she could do anything but tell him the truth.

'My dad was a powerful man,' she said. 'He was at the top of his field and he was wealthy to boot. Very, very wealthy.'

'You know, I figured that,' Henry said dryly and Ginny managed a smile.

'So he had friends all over the world. Friends in most of the major teaching hospitals. Friends in Auckland. The head of medical training for Auckland Central was a house guest here that summer. Dad said he only had to drop a word. He said nursing was a much more suitable profession for someone of Ben's background—his words, not mine. He said it was fine for a kid like Ben to have aspirations and he could have any aspiration he wanted except his daughter. And if he was to keep wanting me then his plans to be a doctor would be pulled from under his feet, just like that. So be a good girl, Ginny, he said. Let him down kindly and move on.'

'So that's what you did.'

'That's what I did,' she said drearily. 'And, of course, he was right. We were only seventeen, and it even seemed sensible. Medical school seemed exciting. The way I was feeling seemed dumb. I managed to dump Ben like it was my idea. But if I'd had the courage to maybe keep writing, keep in touch, who knows? But I couldn't write without crying and then I met James and it was the easy way out. Now I'm so, so sorry.'

There was a long silence, a silence that stretched until she got scared.

'Henry?'

'I'm still here,' he said, almost amicably. 'And Ben could have written, too. Is he sorry?'

'I don't know,' she said, confused.

'Bet he's not,' Henry said. 'He's a guy. I'm seeing a pattern here. I know it's sexist, but *women*. You know, my May once dropped her best meat platter—a plate she inherited from her mum who inherited it from her mum. So she's standing there staring down at five or six bits of broken crockery and she's welling up with tears and saying, oh, Henry, I'm so sorry, I'm so sorry. Like she's apologising to me, or to the shades of her mum and her grandma, but who's hurting? Daft woman. Hell, this piano hurts. You think they're coming?'

'They're coming,' Ginny said, and they were, at least she thought they were. In the distance she could see a Jeep, coming fast. 'At least…I hope…I think Ben's here.'

'Thank God for that,' Henry said morosely. 'A nice shot of morphine'd be useful and I hope he has tin cutters.'

'Or a crane,' Ginny said, hugging Button and climbing to her feet to wave to the approaching Jeep. 'I'm sorry I haven't been more useful.'

'Oh, for heaven's sake, you know where you can put your sorry,' Henry snapped. 'Let's put the past behind us and acknowledge all we both want is Ben.'

CHAPTER NINE

BEN WAS ALONE. Ginny had called for the cavalry and the only one who had come was Ben. That was fine, as far as it went—the hard hug he gave her when he arrived was reassuring, as far as it went—but she wanted more.

Did Wellington have these sorts of problems? Ginny wondered. Did 'Get the fourth infantry division to the front now' mean get them here after the fourth infantry division had finished dinner and put their boots on? Or after the fourth infantry had coped with a wee crisis like fighting five French divisions down the line?

Something must have happened. There must be another catastrophe somewhere, because there was no back-up in sight.

Meanwhile, she and Ben walked carefully around the ruined house, with Ginny carrying Button, while Ben tried to assess how he could get in there.

There seemed no safe way, but Henry's voice, which had risen in hope when Ben had arrived, was now a thready whisper.

And then, appallingly, Henry started to sob.

It wasn't loud sobbing, the kind of wail you'd expect to hear from loss, but the slow rasp of someone in unbearable pain, someone who'd held up as long as he could but had now reached the edge.

'I'm sorry,' he gasped. 'No, don't tell Ginny I said that. I'm not sorry, it's just this damned piano is heavy.'

Ben headed for the radio. 'Where the hell are you guys?'

'The church has come down,' Don barked at him. 'We have three old ladies trapped in the rubble. They were trying to rescue the altar cloths, for heaven's sake, in a building categorised as unsafe. It's okay, we'll get 'em out, but what's worse, the land behind has slipped and our vehicles are trapped. No, it wasn't another tremor, it was just damage we couldn't see—the rise behind the church must have been waiting to fall since the quake. We're organising vehicles on the other side but I reckon it'll be another half-hour before we get up to you.'

'I don't think he can last half an hour,' Ginny whispered. They'd gone back behind Ben's Jeep to radio where Henry couldn't hear. 'Ben, there's a sliver—a small cavity round the back. If you hold Button I could...'

He'd already seen the cavity she was talking about. It was a tiny hump in the caved-in iron. He'd shone his torch in and seen nothing but rubble, but at that point they were only maybe ten feet from where Henry was lying. If they could reach Henry... Even an arm or a leg might be enough to inject painkillers. As well as that, if someone could just be here with him it could make all the difference.

An elderly nurse, an old-school martinet, had instilled *Just being there* into Ben in his first year as an intern.

'Don't be scared of getting personal, Doctor. All these new-fangled drugs and treatments, they don't matter half as much as human contact, and don't you forget it.'

He hadn't. He wasn't forgetting it now.

They'd been talking to Henry—of course they had. Ginny had persuaded Button to sing her favourite song, '*Happy Birthday to Button*', to Henry, and he knew it helped, but touch...

The way Henry sounded…

'You can't,' he said harshly to Ginny. 'I'll go.'

She drew back, appalled. 'No!'

'Hang on. It's okay if you go in but not me?'

'No,' she said, more urgently. 'I'm smaller.'

'And I'm stronger.'

'What if the roof comes down?'

'So what if the roof comes down?' he said. 'Ginny, you know as well as I do that if we don't get drugs on board soon we'll lose him—we can both hear it. I'm only going under iron. You suggested it. I'm the one to do it.'

'No!' It was a cry of terror.

'Yes,' he said. 'Ginny, I'll concede there's a risk. I think it's small but it's still there. With that in mind, I'm a bach-elor with no dependants, and you, my love, like it or not, are a mother with a dependent four-year-old. Your job, I believe, is to keep the home fires burning, take care of the children and prepare slippers and pipe for when your man comes home.'

'Ben!' Despite the gravity of the situation she choked on laughter.

'That's right, my love, I'd like a nice Irish stew when I come out, please, with golden syrup dumplings on the side.' He was shoving gear from his backpack into his pockets as he spoke; syringes and vials, wrapping the vials in dressings to keep them unbroken. Then he gave her a swift, hard kiss, the sort of kiss a man should give his woman as he went off to battle—and he was gone.

She could help him for the first part. At the edge she helped him clear loose rubble, and then as he worked his way under the iron, he shoved stuff sideways and she reached in and helped him haul it clear.

There'd been some sort of sideboard at the side of the

room. It formed a kind of base so the roofing iron hadn't been able to reach floor level.

Once the rubble had been exposed they saw clearly what was happening. The sideboard was too low for Ben to go under it; there was no way they could shift it and neither would they want to—it could bring the whole roof down even further—so Ben had to manoeuvre his way round the sides.

It was filthy, dangerous, even foolhardy, but Henry had grown silent. Ginny had stopped protesting, but she felt sick.

She felt worse when Ben managed to get around the massive sideboard, gave a grunt of satisfaction and hauled himself further under and she could no longer see him. There was now nothing else she could do.

She went back to Button. They started making daisy chains again but Ginny was doing it by feel.

She was watching the crumpled roof and she was watching the track down the valley.

Please, let it not collapse.

Please, let help arrive.

'Talk to me,' she pleaded, and Ben grunted back.

'It's pretty hard to talk with a mouth full of grit. Henry, I know now why we haven't heard from you for a while. You couldn't, I don't know, whistle or something, just to let me know where you are?'

There was a faint attempt at a whistle and Ginny managed a smile and went back to daisy-chain-making as if her life depended on it.

'We need a conversationalist,' Ben grunted, his voice muffled almost to incomprehension. 'Go on, Ginny, tell us a story.'

'Story,' Button said in satisfaction.

Ginny thought, Story? What sort of story?

Ben was inching his way through rubble. Henry was lying trapped in pain. Button was looking up at her expectantly.

She'd been in pressured situations before, but none like this.

Tell us a story.

'Once upon a time,' she said, feeling helpless, and Button beamed and bounced on her knee.

'I like stories.'

'You need to stay quiet,' Ben growled. 'Shush, Button, we all need to hear.'

A story.

Stories don't have to be made up, though, Ginny thought, floundering for inspiration. Stories could be real.

'Once upon a time there was a little girl called Ginny,' she said, and Button squeaked in surprise, but then put her hands firmly across her small mouth as she remembered the rules.

'Ginny's mum and dad brought her to the island but she was very lonely,' Ginny continued. 'She didn't have any friends but she had beautiful clothes.'

'I remember those clothes,' Ben said, muffled, and there was a thump and grating of metal on metal and Ginny's heart almost hit her ankles. But her job wasn't to quiver with fear. She was the storyteller.

'Ginny's mum and dad were busy,' she said. 'They were always busy. So they asked someone else to take care of Ginny. The lady's name was Ailsa and she had a little boy called Ben. The first time Ben met Ginny he pointed to her pretty white pleated skirt and he snickered.'

'I did not,' the voice from under the tin said.

'What's snickered?' Button asked.

'Laughed. He laughed at my white pleated skirt.'

'That wasn't nice,' Button said.

'I didn't think he was a very nice boy,' Ginny agreed. 'But

then he offered to take me tadpoling. You've seen tadpoles, Button. We caught some last week, remember?'

'Yes,' Button said, wiggling more firmly onto Ginny's lap. 'I like this story.'

'As long as I stay the good guy,' Ben said. 'Henry, mate, could you grunt or something? I should be able to see you soon.'

'Grunt,' Henry managed. 'Will that do? Keep going, girl.'

'So he took me tadpoling,' Ginny said. 'Out the back of town there's a farmer's field with a lovely, wide pond. It's a great place for catching taddies.'

'I know it,' Henry said, sounding strained to breaking point. 'You nearly here, lad?'

'Reckon I'm three feet from your feet,' Ben said, sounding just as strained. 'Oi, storyteller, get on with it.'

She couldn't bear it. If the iron came down…if anything happened…

Get on with it.

'So Ben took Ginny to the pond,' she managed. 'And he said the best taddies were on the far side. Now, the farmer had left an old bath lying near the pond. I don't know why, but Ben said it was a good old bath and he used it as a boat. The only problem was there was a hole where the plug should be.'

'Didn't you have a plug?' Ginny asked, and astonishingly Ginny heard Ben chuckle.

'Shush, Button,' he said, mock-sternly. 'This is a very good fairy-tale and I like the ending.'

'Shush yourself,' Ginny said tartly, and it was almost as if he was standing beside her, grinning. Her Ben…

'There was clay by the pond,' she made herself continue. 'So Ben showed Ginny how to make a ball of clay mixed with grass, and shove it into the hole in the bath. Then Ben climbed into the bath and used a pole and pushed himself all the way across the pond and back. He'd obviously done it lots of times because he was very fast.'

'Old trick,' Henry muttered. 'I did that when I was a lad. Got into all sorts of trouble. Hey…'

'Yeah, that's me touching your arm,' Ben said. 'Can you see the flashlight?'

'Can I…? Answer to me prayers,' Henry said, his voice breaking. 'Lad…'

'Hold still. I can reach enough of your arm to give you a shot of something to take the edge off the pain.'

'I'm scared of needles,' Henry retorted, and the old Henry was back. Human contact…the best medicine in the world. Ben was in there with him, and Ginny heard the easing of the old man's terror.

'Be a man and put up with it,' Ben retorted. 'Quick, Ginny, get to the exciting part.'

'So then Ben brought the bathtub back to Ginny's side of the pond,' Ginny said, and for the life of her she couldn't keep her voice steady. 'And Ben made her make her own plug out of clay and grass and fill the hole. And then he pushed her out into the pond and told her how to use the pole to push herself across the pond. The pond wasn't deep but it was very, very muddy. And Ginny wasn't good at rowing. So she was slow, and because she was slow the plug in the bath slowly melted.'

'What does that mean?' Button asked, trying hard to keep up.

'It means,' Ginny said direfully, 'that Ben had tricked Ginny. The hole in the bath was open again and the water was pouring in and Ginny stood in the bath and yelled to Ben to help her but he stood on the bank and laughed while she sank into the mud. And her lovely white pleated skirt got covered with mud, and her pale pink cardigan was ru-ined and her nice curly hair got soaking wet and there was even a tadpole in my…in her hair. And then Ben strode into the pond and rescued…'

'Rescued Ginny,' Button crowed.

'Rescued the tadpole,' Ben said, and even Henry chuckled.

There was a long silence. This was surreal, Ginny thought, sitting in the bright sunlight on this gorgeous autumn morning, where everything seemed perfect, where underneath the ruin one man was fighting for his life and another was putting his life on the line to save him.

'And then did she cry?' Button asked in a small voice, and she had to go back to the story. To how she'd felt as an eight-year-old, standing shoulder deep in mud while this strange boy carefully disengaged a tadpole from her curls. Knowing she'd go home to her parent's disgust. Knowing she'd been tricked. Knowing she looked appalling.

'No,' she said softly, and added, because suddenly it seemed important, 'No, she didn't cry because he saved the tadpole. Just like he's saving Henry now.'

'Oi,' Henry said, and his voice was now sleepy instead of pain-filled. 'Are you comparing me to a tadpole?'

'No,' she said. 'But you're being saved by a hero and all the best stories have heroes.'

'And heroines,' Henry muttered. 'And then they all live happily ever after. Is that you, girl? You're ready for your happy-ever-after?'

'We'll get this roof off you guys first,' she said. 'And then we'll see.'

'That sounds promising,' Ben said, and there was strain in his voice now. What sort of situation was he in? He sounded as if he, too, was in pain. 'So, in your story…the heroine falls in love with her hero?'

'Maybe she did,' she said. 'Maybe he was the first person she'd met who cared more for tadpoles than for pleated skirts.'

'That,' said Henry, 'is just plain weird.'

'Maybe it is,' Ben said. 'But it's important. So the heroine might have fallen in love?'

'The best heroines do,' she whispered.

'Pardon?'

'The best heroines do,' she yelled, and she yelled too loud but it didn't matter. Her Ben was underneath a ruined house, risking his life, and nothing was more important than that.

'A truck's coming,' Button said.

Ginny swivelled and stared down the valley and a truck *was* coming—no, two trucks.

'The cavalry's here,' she told the guys under the house, as she recognised Don Johnson and his fire crew. 'Let's get you guys out and concentrate on fairy-tales later.'

'Let's not forget to,' Ben said. 'I have a feeling the end of this one's pretty import—'

And he got no further.

The aftershock was the biggest yet. It rolled across the island as a great, rolling swell. The iron of the house heaved and shifted.

Ginny heard Ben yell once, just once, and then she had to grab Button and hold her and crouch down until the land settled.

Until the world settled in its next new place.

The fire crew had to stop while the world shook but no more cracks appeared in the earth and as soon as things settled Don ordered his crew forward.

They topped the rise and saw the ruins of Henry's home. A great sheet of roofing iron was ripped almost all the way along and on top of it a woman was tearing at it with her bare hands.

Ginny.

'They're in there,' she screamed at them as Don and his crew reached her. 'Henry and Ben. Ben... The iron's come down. Get it off them. Please, get it off them. I can't bear it. Oh, Ben... Oh, Ben, my love, no...'

If it hadn't been for the dust they would have been fine. Or sort of fine. The world gave a giant heave, the mass of iron and debris above them rolled and shook and shuddered, there was momentary pressure on Ben's chest that took his breath away but then the iron shifted again and the pressure eased—and the heaving stopped.

He was fine except the torch had rolled somewhere out of reach, beaming a useless stream of light into unreachable darkness. The air was clogged with a dust so thick he couldn't breathe and Henry was rasping with ever-decreasing strength.

What was it they said in planes? Fit your own mask first and then help others around you?

First make a mask.

He was trying to haul his shirt off but there wasn't enough room to manoeuvre. He needed to rip the thing and who would have guessed how strong shirts were? Note: remember to buy cheaper ones. He couldn't get his hands apart wide enough to wrench it.

He had a sudden flash of memory of Ginny's shirt ripping...how many hours ago?

Ginny.

Above him he could hear her sobbing, ripping away at the tin, her voice filled with terror. He wanted to reassure her, to tell her he'd be fine, but he wasn't yet. It was so hard to breathe.

Finally the shirt gave way, and he wrenched again, haul-

ing the arms off so he had two long strips and large panels
front and back.

What followed was more ripping and then wriggling in
the darkness, trying to get cloth on his face and the sleeves
around to tie his makeshift mask on. But when he did, the
relief was almost instant. The appalling, clogging muck was
kept out by the barrier.

Now for Henry.

'Ben? Henry?' Ginny was screaming from above but there
was no way he could use precious air to call back. He had
to get closer to Henry. He had to.

He heaved himself forward, risked bringing the entire
sheet of rubble down on them, but he had no choice. Before
it had simply been enough to reach Henry, to get the drugs
to his arm, but now he had to get to his face; he had to fit a
mask. The drugs he'd given him would depress his breathing still more.

He was hauling at the rubble, pushing forward—and miraculously something moved, gave and he could pull himself
the last foot forward and feel Henry's head.

'Mate…Henry?'

He got no answer—Henry's entire focus was on his weak,
rasping breaths.

'Help me, Henry,' Ben managed, and swept a handful
of dust from the old man's face and somehow managed to
get the back of his shirt across it. He was clearing Henry's
mouth, shifting muck the old man was clearly unable to shift
himself. 'Breathe through the cloth. Breathe…'

'They're coming, Ben, they're coming,' Ginny called from
above, and he gave up trying to tie Henry's mask in place. It
was too hard. He didn't have enough breath left himself. He
simply lay full length in the filth and held Henry's makeshift mask in position and willed Henry to keep on living.

Ginny'd tell them where he was. Ginny'd bring in the troops.

Ginny…

The thought of her up there in the sunlight was his one true thing. He thought of her again as she'd been at eight years old, standing in tadpole territory, and he thought how he'd decided he had been stupid asking her to marry him when he'd been seventeen.

He should have asked when he was eight.

'Just keep breathing, mate,' he told Henry. 'Just keep on breathing, one breath after another. Over and over. Breathe, breathe, breathe, because Ginny's up there waiting for us, and I, for one, have unfinished business with the lady. I suspect she loves us both and, dammit, I suspect if we die she'll blame herself. She's dumb like that, but there it is. For Ginny's sake, we keep on breathing.'

Don's crew consisted of eight emergency workers, tough, work-ready men and women who were trained to cope with stuff just like this, a few who'd been in earthquakes before, who understood about risk and urgency. This was no massive collapse of stone. It simply needed strength, skill and the right equipment, all of which they had.

Ginny had been trying to haul sheets of iron back from where she'd last heard voices. Don put her aside, snapped a few incisive questions and then set his crew to work.

In less than five minutes the vast sheets of tin were rolling back, exposing what was beneath.

What was there was a massive pile of rubble, dust, grit— and two prone bodies, one almost completely covering the other.

For one appalling moment Ginny thought they were both dead. She'd backed to the edge of the ruin to give the guys space to move but she hadn't been able to take her eyes from what was being exposed.

Two bodies…

And then one raised his head, revealing a makeshift mask and a face so caked in dust it was unrecognisable. But, of course, she recognised it.

Ben.

'I'm fine,' he said in a voice that wasn't the least bit fine; it was the merest croak through the mask. 'And I reckon Henry'll be okay, too, once we get this piano off his leg.'

And miraculously there was a grunt of agreement from Henry.

Ben was hauled to safety first. They tugged him to his feet, he staggered but then stood, unhurt, whole.

Ginny started breathing again. She hadn't been aware she'd stopped but her body sucked in air like she'd been drowning.

Ben. Safe.

He didn't come to her. Instead, he watched as four strong men, one at each corner of the piano, acting in unison, lifting the thing clear. And Henry was out, free.

There was stuff to do. Somehow she shifted into doctor mode, adding to Ben's in-the-dark care, setting up IV lines while Ben snapped orders to keep Henry's spine steady, watch for his hips and beware of a possible broken pelvis as they transferred him to a rigid stretcher to carry him back across the ruins.

But Henry was giving sleepy directions himself. 'When are you going to get a tarp here to cover this? There's stuff here worth saving. Be careful of that piano.'

And Ginny knew, she just knew, that he'd be fine.

Finally, finally there was time for Ben to turn to her, for Ben to take her in his arms, to hug her close.

'About time,' Henry said weakly from his stretcher. 'We've only been waiting twelve years for this to happen.'

There was laughter, filled with relief, but Ginny hardly heard it. Ben had her in his arms, against his heart. Her world folded into his; into him. Heart against heart.

He kissed her hair and then he tilted her chin and he kissed her on the mouth, a full, public proclamation that this was his woman, his love.

She melted into him. This proclamation was okay by her. What were her qualms anyway? Last night had been the beginning of the rest of her life. Why had she ever thought she wasn't brave enough to start again?

How could she not when that start was Ben?

There was slow clapping. Somehow they broke apart and found everyone was looking at them, cheering, and Henry was even leading the clapping from his stretcher.

Ben smiled and smiled at her. Her love. Her Ben.

And then he looked around, still smiling, and said, 'Where's Button?'

She'd forgotten Button. In the midst of her terror her thoughts hadn't swerved from the two men fighting for their lives in the ruins. When the second tremor had hit she'd almost thrown Button into the Jeep. She'd said stay, and she'd run.

But now…

She was standing in the arms of Ben, who was safe, safe, safe, and a little girl who depended solely on her was no longer where she'd left her.

Ginny was no longer in Ben's arms. She was staring wildly around her.

'Button!' Her yell sounded out over the valley, echoing back and back and back.

The Jeep was empty. She stared back at the ruins. Surely she would have seen… If Button had come anywhere near the ruins, she would have noticed.

She should have noticed. What sort of a mother…?

The cliff…

But Ben was before her.

'Button's missing,' he snapped to the team around him. 'Four years old. Priority one.'

Triage… When faced with an emergency, take time to assess then look at worst-case scenarios first. That meant no matter who was yelling, who was bleeding, you took the time to assess, see the guy with the grey face clutching his chest, know that even though it might simply be shock and bruising you checked that out first.

So head for worst-case scenarios first. The worst scenario was that Button was buried under the debris…but maybe it wasn't. Because Ben was turning away from the ruin and striding—no, running—towards the cliff.

The cliff. Dear God.

Below was the sea, fascinating, awesome for a little girl who had no sense of danger.

Ginny gave a sob of terror and followed, but Ben was before her.

He reached the edge.

'Here,' he snapped back at them. 'She's slipped down a bit but there's a ledge. Button, don't move. Sweetheart, I want you to play statues, don't move at all. I'm coming down.'

And just as he said it a tiny tremor, the vaguest hint of an aftershock, rocked the world. It may have been tiny but it was too much for what must have already been a weakened stretch of headland.

A crack opened between Ginny and Ben. A tiny crack, but it was widening.

Ben gave a yell of warning. 'Ginny, stay where you are.'

And then he slid over the edge of the cliff, helpless, as the crack widened still further and the land seemed to slide toward the sea.

What did you do when your life crumpled before your eyes?
Nothing?
There was nothing she could do. She stood numb with shock and terror while around her men and women leapt into action.

They'd been in earthquakes before? Disasters? They must have been for instead of standing like useless idiots they had ropes out of the truck, they were gearing up with harnesses and shackles, and Don was edging out to where the edge of the cliff was a crumpling mess of loose dirt.

Someone was holding onto her, a woman who seemed just as competent as the men but whose job, obviously, was to keep her out of harm's way.

'We're belaying down,' she told Ginny. 'Hold on, love, Don's good. If anyone can reach them, he can.'

The world held its breath. There was no way anyone else could go near the edge—the headland was still crumbling, and another tremor could hit at any moment.

Don edged out, slowly, slowly. Dirt was breaking away as he moved, but he was testing the footing each time before putting his weight on it. He was safe; they'd fastened the rope onto the Jeep and the crew was guiding it to keep it steady but the last thing they wanted was to cause further collapse.

And then Don was over the edge and lower, lower.

'They're here.' His voice crackled through the radio. 'Send down two harnesses, a big 'un and a little 'un. The kid looks okay and Ben's holding her. Ben's shoved Button against the cliff face. He looks in pain—he's hit something but he's conscious. He's kept her safe from the landfall. Harnesses fast would be good. It'd be a bit of a waste to lose them now.'

A bit of bruising and confusion—that was Button.

One fractured pelvis—that was Henry.

Pain, dropping blood pressure, possible internal injuries, that was Ben. Ginny set up IV lines, gave him pain relief, tried desperately to be a doctor rather than a woman whose man was in mortal danger.

They called in the chopper, and Dave, the doctor Ginny had met the night before, came with it. Dave took over from Ginny, examining Ben fast, concurring with what she thought—or hoped. Was it foolish to hope for the best? 'Query ruptured spleen,' Dave barked into the radio—there were directives to take them straight to Auckland—and then there was nothing Ginny could do but hold Button and try to stop shaking.

'Take Ginny down to the med centre,' Dave told the team as the chopper prepared to take off. 'She'll need something for shock.'

'I don't,' Ginny said as she watched the chopper lift. She'd said goodbye to Henry—and to Ben—but it had all been done in such a rush there'd been no time to talk. Ben had taken her hand and gripped hard, but she wasn't sure if it had been need or pain making him hold on so tight.

She wanted, so much, to go with him, but her priority had to be Button.

She'd forgotten Button once. Not again.

She felt sick to the depths of her soul.

'You idiot.' She heard James's voice echo back to her, words that had been said over and over in their marriage. 'You don't have the brains you were born with.'

She stood in the morning sun and let the words play and replay.

It was her fault that Ben could be so hurt.

Even Henry… She should have insisted he stay with her at the vineyard. She should have…

'Come on, Ginny, let's get you down to the hospital,' Don said, and she shook her head.

'I'm fine,' she said dully. 'No thanks to me, but Button and I are okay. I can still drive. Thank you all for your care, but I need to manage by myself.'

'On a scale of one to ten, how bad's the pain?' Dave asked Ben as the chopper headed out over the sea.

'Eleven,' Ben said morosely, and then at Dave's look of alarm he shook his head. 'Sorry. Seven, I guess, so, yes, I would like a top-up. There's just a few more things going on.'

'Like leaving his lady,' Henry said from beside him. They'd set both patients up with headphones so they could speak to each other. 'He'll be feeling bad because of Ginny.'

'Ginny seems okay,' Dave said, startled. 'She's a competent woman.'

'Yeah, she's a competent woman and a fine doctor,' Ben managed through his pain. 'But the lady has demons. I thought I'd slayed enough of them to break through, but something tells me Henry and I have conjured up a whole lot more.'

She drove carefully back into town, filling her mind with plans, figuring how she needed to get the house inspected and repaired, get the manager's residence liveable for Henry, persuade Henry to stay, get her and Button back to the vineyard.

Her list was vast, and she concentrated on it fiercely, because if she didn't concentrate, fears broke in. As well as that, the voices flooded back, accusing, and it was too hard to cope with.

She'd had a whole lifetime of not being good enough, and she was weary to the bone.

'I am good enough,' she said out loud, finally cracking and letting the voices hold sway. Trying to defend herself by facing them down. 'I will look after Button. I will.'

'And that's all,' she added in a less fierce voice, a voice that was an acknowledgment that she couldn't fight failure on more than one front. 'That's all I'm focussing on. I might love Ben. I might even love medicine, but I stuff things up and I won't risk it any further. I'll help Ben with emergency medicine until he finds someone else but that's all. It's Button and the vineyard and nothing else.'

CHAPTER TEN

A WEEK LATER Ben went out to the vineyard to find her. When he arrived Ginny was hammering boards onto the veranda of the vineyard manager's residence. Button had a hammer as well and was banging everything in sight. Ginny paused in her hammering as the car approached, but Button kept right on going.

His mother had driven him up from the town. She paused at the gate—there seemed to be unstable ground along the driveway and she wasn't risking driving further—and looked at the woman and child in front of them.

'You sure you want to do this? Do you want me to wait?' she asked.

'Nope,' he said. 'Ginny will drive me back.'

'You might have trouble getting her out of here,' Ailsa said worriedly. 'Okay, it's not the shaky ground I'm worried about. I know you can go cross-country. But she's wounded and retreating, Ben. More wounded even than you are.'

'What, worse than a ruptured spleen?'

'You don't have a spleen any more and Ginny still has her wounds,' Ailsa said sternly. 'Her father was a bully and a thug, and her mother was appalling. I know you love her but even when she was a kid I could see her shadows. From what I hear, her marriage has just meant longer ones.'

'I can cope with shadows,' Ben said, but uneasily because he wasn't sure that he could.

'Good luck,' his mother said, and leaned across and kissed him before he climbed out of the truck, carrying his grandfather's old walking cane for support. His ruptured spleen had been removed by laparoscopic surgery, he was recovering nicely but he'd been bruised just about everywhere it was possible for a man to be bruised. His mother had been fussing, and maybe she had cause.

'Give me a ring if you don't get anywhere,' she said now, and glanced ahead at Ginny. 'You might need more than a walking stick to get through this pain.'

'If I travelled by helicopter to Auckland with a ruptured spleen, I can get through anything,' Ben said, but Ailsa still looked doubtful as she drove away.

Ginny had seen him arrive. She'd started walking towards them, pausing to fetch Button. It seemed Button wasn't to be allowed out of her sight.

She stopped coming towards him when Ailsa drove away.

'H-hi,' she managed, and then the doctor part of her took over. 'Surely you shouldn't be out here, walking. I… Can I get you a chair?'

'I'm fine,' Ben said, and then they both looked at the walking stick. 'And I'm tough,' he said, like he was convincing himself. He managed a grin. 'Chairs are for wusses. Thanks for the flowers.'

'They were…the least I could do.'

'And you always do the least you can do? That's Hannah's line, not yours.'

They were twenty yards apart. It was slow going with his walking stick—he had a corked thigh that was still giving him hell a week after the event—and Ginny had stopped and wasn't coming any closer. 'I thought you might visit,' he said. 'I sort of hoped.'

'I phoned.'

'To enquire. And then didn't ask to be put through. Coward.'

'On the card I said I was sorry,' Ginny managed. 'There didn't seem anything else to say. I *am* sorry, Ben. I can't say more than that. So why would you want to see me?'

'To ask you to marry me.'

Marry...

The word was huge. The word was impossible, Ben thought as he watched all the colour drain from her face. Maybe his plan to put it all out there hadn't been such a good idea after all.

'Ben...'

'What happened wasn't your fault,' he said. 'Nothing's your fault. You're my Ginny and I'm your Ben. Bad things happen but whenever they do, we face them together.'

'You wouldn't want to share...my bad things.'

'Ginny...'

'I always get it wrong,' she blurted out. 'I try and try but it never turns out right. Even Button...I'm so scared of caring for Button. I know she has no choice. I know she needs me, but she'd be so much better with someone who can love without messing things up.'

'That sounds...' He sorted his words carefully, fighting for the right ones. 'As if you're seriously thinking of stepping away.'

'I can't,' she said. 'Not from Button.'

'And from me?'

'Yes,' she said. 'From you.' It was a bald, harsh statement, and he thought suddenly of the harsh things Ginny had said to him when she'd been seventeen, and how he'd believed her and had let her go.

It'd be easier to be a caveman, he thought suddenly. It'd be over the shoulder, a bit of manly exercise lugging her back to his lair and he'd have her for the rest of her life. But now…he had to make her see sense.

'Do you love me?' He asked it like it was the most natural question in the world, like it was totally reasonable for a guy who ought to be in bed to lean on his walking stick in the midday sun and wait for an answer to a question of such import that it took his breath away.

But there'd never be a better time to say it, he thought.

Maybe there'd never be a good time to say it.

He watched the doubts flash across her face, the fear, and he drove his advantage.

'Yes, my first question was marriage,' he conceded. 'That didn't get me anywhere, so let's try this from a different angle. No lies, Ginny. Do you love me?'

'Too…too much,' she whispered.

He nodded. 'As a matter of interest, did you love me when I was seventeen?'

'Yes, but—'

'So what Henry told me was true. We shared a ward in Auckland and he told me. You tossed me over because your old man made threatening noises about my career.'

'He shouldn't have told—'

'Henry shouldn't have told me?'

'No.'

It was too much, he thought. He was aching all over. She was standing there in her faded jeans, dirty from pruning grapes, holding Button's hand, and she was just as unattainable as she'd been at seventeen. Dammit, did she really expect him to walk away?

'Henry shouldn't have told?' Suddenly he was practically shouting—okay, he was shouting, and he might frighten Button but Button looked interested rather than scared. 'Henry shouldn't have told? What about you? Why didn't you say it like it was and we could have faced it down together? You don't need to fight shadows yourself. Think about the immorality of your father's threats. Think about the sheer cowardly bullying of your husband, the guy who's making you shrink now and look like a scared rabbit because some-how you think it's all your fault that I'm angry. Do you love me, Ginny?'

'Yes, but—'

'Then that's all I need right now,' he said grimly. 'Go take a shower. We're going to a funeral.'

'Ben...'

'If you think I'm letting you lock yourself away all over again, you have another think coming,' he snapped. 'I shouldn't be here. I'm incapable of driving. I'm walking wounded standing in your driveway and I promised Squid that I'd speak at his funeral.' He glanced at his watch. 'In forty minutes from now. So Hannah's meeting us at the church to take care of Button and you're going to get yourself into something a wee bit cleaner and then you're driving me to the funeral. And then you're coming in with me, Ginny, like it or not. You're part of this island. I need you, Ginny.'

And then he softened as he saw her face. She looked like a deer trapped in headlights, but he wouldn't—he couldn't—let her walk away.

'I can't do this alone, Ginny,' he said, and he held out his hand. 'One step at a time. I won't talk marriage. I won't even push the love bit, but I will push belonging. Squid knew you as an islander, as do I. You were with us when we needed you most. This is to say farewell to one of us. Ginny, come with me, just for now.'

'You mean you come with me,' she said with an attempt at humour. 'I appear to have the only set of wheels here.'

'That's why I need you, Ginny, love,' he said. 'That and

about fifty other reasons and a lot more besides. Come on, love, it's a date you can't refuse. Let's go and say goodbye to Squid.'

She sat in a pew at the back of the crowded church. Ailsa squashed in with her and gave her a swift hug.

'Ben's been asked to do the eulogy,' she said. 'He and Squid were friends. He's feeling it.'

And she fell silent as if she was feeling it, too, and Ginny was left with her own thoughts.

Love? Marriage?

She'd just hurt him, as she'd hurt him already.

That had been her cowardice talking. That had been the shades of her parents and James.

But to hurt someone else…to expose Ben to mistakes she'd inevitably make? How could she do that?

Ailsa's hand gripped hers.

'He loves you with all his heart,' she whispered. 'Go on, Ginny, love, jump.'

Was she so obvious? She dredged up a half-hearted smile as they rose for the first hymn.

Jump? And that was all she had to do. Jump, dragging Ben with her. And what was at the base of that leap?

The hymn ended. Ben was in front of the congregation, in front of the plain, wooden coffin, holding a sheet of paper before him. 'Squid asked me to speak today,' he said, and her heart turned over. 'And everyone here knows Squid. He liked to predict what would happen so he made sure. He wrote this just before the earthquake, just in case, telling me exactly what to say.'

There was a ripple of laughter, and then the room fell silent. Squid had been an ancient fisherman, a constant presence on the waterfront since childhood, and the island would be the poorer for his going. Besides, who would predict disaster now?

'It wasn't my fault.'

Ben's first words—Squid's first words—hauled Ginny from nostalgia and regret. They were her words, she thought in confusion—or maybe they weren't.

She'd spent a childhood trying to desperately defend herself with those words—*it wasn't my fault*—only to learn it was easier to appease and accept.

It was my fault.

'"Me heart's been giving me trouble for a couple of years now",' Ben read, following faithfully the script on the page. Unconsciously, his voice even sounded a little like Squid's. '"Doc's been telling me I ought to go to mainland to get one of those valve replacement thingies but, sheesh, I'm ninety-seven—I might be even older when you hear this—and who wants stuff inside you that don't belong.

'"So I'm sitting on the wharf enjoying me last days in the sun and I'm starting to tell all you fellas there's a big 'un coming. An earthquake. Be good if it did, I'm thinking, only to prove me right, but I sort of hope I'm wrong. Only then I'm reading in the papers there's two scientist fellas somewhere who are in jail because they didn't predict an earthquake and I reckon the world's gone mad. If I'm wrong then it's my fault? If I'm right is it my fault 'cos I didn't yell at you louder? Fault. Like Doc telling me I need a new valve. Is it his fault I'm lying in this damned coffin?"'

There was a ripple of uneasy laughter through the church. Ginny had heard the island whispers, and sometimes the voices had risen higher than whispers. 'Someone should have warned us. Who can we sue?'

She thought of James, apoplectic with fury because she'd tried to inject a drug he'd needed and had had trouble finding a vein. Lashing out at her. 'It's your fault I'm in this mess.'

It was totally irrational, but blame was a powerful tool. When all else failed, find someone to blame.

"'You want me to cop it so you'll all feel better?'" Squid—Ben—said from the pulpit. "'No way. That's what I want to say here. That's the reason I didn't ask to get wrapped in a tarp and tipped over the side of me fishing boat out at sea before I'd had this nice little ceremony. I reckon if I'm right about the quake and it sets me ticker off—and I know it might—you might be sitting here shaking your fist at me coffin, saying the mad old coot caused this mess.

"'So I just wanted to say stuff it, no one causes earth-quakes so don't dare stop drinking beer at me wake if it's happened. I want a decent wake and I want you to pour a bit of beer over me coffin and then toss me out to sea with no regrets and say I'm done. Great life. Great times. Great is-land. Merv Larkin, notes on me snapper spot are written on the back of the calendar of me dunny. That's it, then. There's me legacy. See you.'"

Ben paused then. There were more ripples of laughter but Ginny still heard the odd murmur. There had been blame. Ben was watching calmly as islanders elbowed each other.

She knew the mutterings. 'If Squid knew, why didn't he say just how bad it'd be? Why didn't he talk to the main-land scientists, shove it down their throats, get official warn-ings out?'

'He really didn't know.' It was Ben now, Ben speaking his own words, and suddenly he was looking at Ginny. Straight at Ginny. He was smiling faintly, and suddenly she knew that his smile was meant only for her.

'A hundred years of living, and you know what Squid knew for sure?' Ben said. 'That no one knows a sausage. We can make guesses and we make them all the time. I'll cross this road because chances are a meteor's not going to drop on my head. That's a guess. It's a pretty good guess, and Squid's earthquake prediction was a pretty good guess, too, backed up by a hundred years of Squid's grandpa telling him the signs. But, still, unless Squid got underground and heaved, it wasn't his fault.

'Meteors are sitting over everyone's head and one day they'll drop, nothing surer, and we just need to accept it. Anyway that's all I need to say except we were blessed to have Squid. We should have no regrets except that even though he's left his snapper spots, his best crayfish spots die with him. We loved him, he drove us nuts and we'll miss him. That's pretty much all we need to say, except he left enough money for everyone to have a beer or a whisky on him. Bless him.'

There was laughter, but this time it wasn't uncomfortable. There was the odd sniff and the organist belted out a mighty rendition of what must surely be the island's favourite hymn by the strength of the island voices raised in farewell.

And then six weathered fishermen led by a limping Ben carried the coffin from the church, the hearse carried the coffin down to the wharf because after all this he would be buried at sea—and then the island proceeded to the pub.

'Shall we join them?' Ailsa asked, and Ginny realised Ailsa had been holding her hand all the time. Even while singing.

As if Ginny was her daughter?

She wasn't this woman's daughter.

She could be.

Courage.

'I'm a wimp,' she said softly, and Ailsa followed her gaze to where Ben was talking to the pallbearers while they watched the hearse drive slowly through the still rubble-strewn streets down to the harbour.

'You trusted,' Ailsa said. 'You trusted your father and

you trusted your husband. It's no fault to trust, child. But you know Ben would never hurt you.'

'It's not that. I just...mess things up.'

'Like Squid messed the island up,' Ailsa said briskly. 'Nonsense. You want to take that attitude, then you are a wimp. Get a grip, girl, go for what you want and stand up for yourself. Now, you want to head for the pub for a bit of Dutch courage? Squid's prepaid for the very best beer—and whisky all round.'

'I need to think,' Ginny said, and Ailsa shook her head and tugged her forward.

'Nonsense, girl. You need to belong.'

CHAPTER ELEVEN

BEN AND THE pallbearers accompanied the coffin out to sea. Ginny headed to the pub and ordered a glass of Squid's excellent whisky but only one, she told herself, because she really did have some thinking to do.

Serious thinking.

She was an accepted part of the island, she thought. No one looked askance at her; in fact, she was being treated with affection.

'Word is you've had a rough time of it,' one of the farmers who lived beyond her vineyard said. 'Doc says we're to leave you be, no pressure, but don't you bury yourself too long, girl. We need you.'

'I know the island needs a doctor...'

'Not just that,' the man said. 'I know this sounds dumb but you're an islander. You always seemed one, not like your mum and dad, but even when you were a little tacker it was like you were coming home every time you came here. And we don't like losing islanders.'

He stared into his beer and gave a rueful smile. 'We don't even like losing ninety-seven-year-olds who smell like smoked mackerel and prophesy doom. We'll miss him, like we're missing you, girl. Doctor or not, this is your home.'

There wasn't a lot she could say after a speech like that.

She hadn't brought enough tissues. Dratted funerals. Dratted islanders.

Dratted Ben.

She took her whisky and escaped out through the beer garden, through the back gate she and Ben had sneaked through when they had been under age, then out along the path that led to the island's best swimming beach.

It had barely been damaged by the quake. A few rocks had rolled down the gentle slope but the path was fine. She headed down, slipped off her shoes and went and sat on a rock and stared out to sea. Towards the mainland.

You're an islander.

She was crying good and proper now. There weren't enough tissues in the world for how she was crying, and she didn't care.

She didn't cry. Until she'd come back to the island she'd never cried. Not once, not at her father's funeral, not once when James had been diagnosed and died. So why was crying now?

Who knew? She didn't. She was so out of control she felt like she was falling, and when Ben sat down beside her and put his arm around her and pulled her into him, she had no strength to pull away.

She was falling and he was the only thing stopping her.

He took the whisky glass carefully out of her hand—the thing was half-full and one part of her still acknowledged it was excellent whisky and Squid would probably haunt her if she spilled it. Ben set it on the rock beside them, and then he carefully turned her towards him and tugged her into his arms.

'I…I'm soggy,' she managed, and it was almost impossible to get that much out.

'You're allowed to cry at funerals.'

'I don't.'

'Because you're not allowed to?'

'I don't cry. I won't cry,' she said, and cried some more, and the front of his shirt was soaked and she was being ridiculous and she couldn't stop.

'I'm...I'm sorry...'

'Ginny...' He hauled back from her then, held her at arm's length, and his face was suddenly as grim as death. 'Don't.'

'Don't...'

'Don't you dare apologise,' he snapped. 'Not once. You know what you did when I sank your bathtub?'

'I threw...I threw mud at you.' How did people speak through tears? It looked so elegant in the movies—here it felt like she was talking through a snorkel.

'And very appropriate it was, too,' Ben said, the sternness replaced by the glimmer of a smile. 'And then?'

'And then you said if I didn't tell your mum what you'd done, you'd give me your best taddy—the one that looked like it'd be a bullfrog to beat all bullfrogs.'

'A supreme sacrifice,' he said nobly. 'And I watched you care for him and skite about him to the other kids...'

'I did not skite!'

'You skited. And then I watched you let him go—my bullfrog—and I swear he or his descendants are around here still, thinking they owe their whole family lineage to you. That pond was full of ducks. He'd have been a goner but you were his lifesaver and not me. You know what? I should have just said sorry and kept the bullfrog for myself. But I didn't feel sorry. I felt...' He smiled at her then, a killer smile that had wobbled her heart when at eight years old and was wobbling her heart still.

'I felt like it was the way things were,' he said. 'I covered you with mud so you got to raise my bullfrog. But you know what? I loved watching you raise my bullfrog. There wasn't a single bit of sorry left in there.'

'Ben...'

'If we married,' he said, and the smile had gone again. 'That's what I'd want. Not one single bit of sorry.'

'You can't want to marry me,' she whispered. 'To take me on with all my baggage. To help raise another man's child...'

'It's like the bullfrog,' he said softly. 'You'd give your baggage to me and I'd take it on and you'd watch me care for it and it'd be like caring for it yourself. That's the way I see it. That's the way it's always been for us, Ginny. Not a single sorry between us, now and for ever.'

'But I hurt you.'

'And I pressured you. Pushing a seventeen-year-old to marry me... We both needed a life before we settled down. It seems like I've had a happier one—I've had some very nice girlfriends, thank you very much, all of whom sound nicer than your creepier James, but I'd prefer if you don't ask me about them, and you can tell me as much or as little about James as you want. All I'll tell you about my girlfriends is that not a single one of them would have raised my tadpole into the fine specimen of a bullfrog he turned out to be. So no sorry, Ginny. Get every tear you need to shed, shed them now and then move forward.'

She couldn't talk. What was it with tears? If she was Audrey Hepburn she'd have whisked away the last teardrop from her beautiful eyelashes and would now be fluttering said eyelashes up at her love.

Where were tissues?

'Here,' Ben said, and handed over a man-sized handkerchief.

'A handkerchief,' she said, sidetracked. 'A handkerchief?'

'I never go to a funeral without one,' he said. 'You'll note the left-hand corner is already a little doggy.'

She choked and he tugged her close again and then he simply held her; he held her and held her until finally she sort of dried up and she sort of pulled herself together and she sort of thought…that this was okay.

That this was where she belonged.

That this was home.

But to let go of the baggage of years? To let go of sorry?

'If you're still harping on sorry, then I see your duty is to catch me a very big tadpole for a wedding gift,' Ben said, putting her away from him again.

And she choked again. 'How did you know what I was thinking?'

'I just do. I always did. Like you know me, my love. You know we fit. Maybe it's time we acknowledged it.'

'Button…Button might like to be a flower girl,' she said, and his face stilled.

'I didn't know you were thinking that.'

'I'm thinking all sorts of things,' she admitted. 'So many things you can't possibly keep up.'

'So one of them might be that you'd marry me?'

'Only if I can get braver.'

'You're brave already,' he said steadily. 'You took Button on without a backward look. You didn't walk away from James, no matter how he treated you. It's not bravery that's missing, my love. It's the ability to stand over a smashed vase or a broken leg or a patient we lost no matter how we worked to save him and say, "This is life." That's all it is, life. It'll throw bad things at us, you and I both know that, but it'll also throw joy. Joy, joy and more joy if you'll marry me.'

'Ben—'

'You weren't responsible for James' death. You know that,' he said. 'Say it.'

'I wasn't responsible.'

'Or for your father's death or for his disappointment that you didn't win the Nobel Prize before he died.'

'I guess…'

'And your mother's appalling disappointment that you turned out not to be blonde.'

'Hey, I wouldn't go that far,' she said, suddenly realising her tears had gone. She wasn't sure what was taking their place—some emotion she'd never felt before. Liberation?

Freedom?

'It was a heinous crime not to be blonde,' she managed, and Ben grinned.

'Yes, it was. So can you stand in the dock, look your accusers in the face and say it wasn't your fault?'

'I guess.'

'You want to have fun?'

'Fun,' she said, and the word was weird. Foreign.

'I'm not marrying you unless you turn back into the Ginny I knew,' he said. He motioned to the gently sloping rise behind the beach. The earthquake had shaken free a great swathe of loose, soft sand. It looked…sort of poised.

Poised to slide straight down the slope into the shallows beneath it.

'The Ginny I know would ride that slope,' Ben said.

'I'd get wet.'

'You're already soggy.'

'So I am.' She looked at him, her gorgeous, kind, clever Ben, her love who'd magically waited for her for all this time, who'd made her see what she should have been yelling at the top of her lungs for years.

'I believe I'm about to burst a few chains,' she said, and Ben looked startled.

'Pardon?'

'You don't know what you're getting into. If it's not my fault I'll break cups all over the place. And…' she eyed the sandy slope thoughtfully '…I'll get sand in my knickers. But I won't do it alone.'

'I don't want you to do anything alone any more,' he said,

and then added a hasty rider. 'Within reason. It seems to me you've been on your own all your life. You hook up with me, you have a whole island. We're part of a community but we're a team. You and me, Dr Koestrel. Together for ever.'

'Prove it,' she said, and he blinked.

'What?'

'Remember all those years ago when I wanted to be your friend. Prove it, you said, by rowing this bathtub all the way across the pond.'

'Haven't we moved on from that?'

'Maybe you have,' she said. 'But I'm still wary. See this slope? It's gentle sand—a gentle slope. It shouldn't hurt someone who had his surgery laprascopically and I'll kiss the bruises. Together or nothing, Dr McMahon.'

'I'll get sand in *my* knickers.'

'Yes, you will,' she said serenely, because suddenly she was serene. She was happy, she thought incredulously. She was totally, awesomely happy. She was in love, in love, in love, and miraculously the man she loved was smiling at her, loving her right back, and all she was asking was that he slide on a little sand for her.

She thought of the impossibility of asking either of her parents to do such a thing, or James, and she wondered why she hadn't seen it? The fault had never been in her. It had been in them. They'd chosen the wrong daughter, the wrong wife. Their perfect daughter, perfect wife was maybe out there somewhere but it wasn't her, and whoever it was who wanted to be blonde and perfect and servile, well, good luck to them. It wasn't her.

'Slide or nothing,' she said.

'You will kiss the bruises? Slide and everything?' Ben asked, and that gorgeous twinkle was back, the twinkle she'd first met twenty years ago, the Ben twinkle, of mischief, life and laughter.

'Everything,' she said, and turned and headed up the sand bank, and she knew he'd follow.

And he did.

Two minutes later two very wet, very sandy doctors emerged from a shallow wave, laughing and spluttering, and Ben was holding Ginny and Ginny was holding Ben, and she knew that here was her home.

Here was her love. Her life. Her whole.

And then—after all the bruises had been very satisfactorily kissed and a few other places besides—because it seemed like the right time, the right place, the right everything, Ben took Ginny's hand and led her back to the pub. Squid's wake was just starting to wind up but most of the islanders were still there.

They turned to stare in amazement at the picture of the two sodden island doctors, Ben's suit dripping, Ginny even wearing a bit of seaweed.

They stood in the doorway and Ben held Ginny's hand tightly while the voices faded and every eye was on them.

'We have an announcement to make,' Ben said to the whole pub, the whole island, the whole world. 'I'd like to tell everyone who's listening that Ginny has just agreed to marry me. And, Squid, if you're listening up there, no, it's not your fault but you lent a hand. The lady loves me, ladies and gentleman, and the next ceremony on this island's going to be a wedding.'

And so it was.

Ginny's wedding to James had taken place in Sydney's biggest cathedral, with a luxury reception in a lush ballroom overlooking Sydney Harbour.

Ginny's wedding to Ben took place in the small island chapel where they'd said goodbye to Squid, and the reception took place on the beach.

Simple, Ginny had decreed, but she didn't quite have her way. The islanders prepared a party to end all parties. Ailsa made her a dress that was breathtakingly lovely, with a sweetheart neckline, a cinched waist and a skirt that flowed out in a full circle if she spun.

And she did spin, as Ben took her into his arms and proceeded to jive instead of doing a bridal waltz.

'You can't waltz on sand,' he decreed, and she didn't think she could jive on sand either, but it seemed she could.

And did.

So did Button, dressed in a gorgeous pink dress the same style as Ginny's, jiving along with Henry, who was enjoying himself very much indeed. He was back living in the manager's residence at the vineyard now, pottering in the vineyard, falling in love with Button, deeply content with the way life was turning out. Looking forward to Ben and Ginny and Button sharing the big house.

He'd decreed Button was now his family, as was the tiny black and white kitten that followed Button everywhere. As for Button, she was pretty much in heaven. The heart specialist had decided surgery would be necessary to repair a slight abnormality but it could wait, he said. No rush. No drama. For now they could settle into what they were.

Family.

The islanders had lit the campfire to beat all campfires. Dusk was settling into night. The local band was playing its collective heart out, there was enough food for a small army, people were dancing, singing, gossiping, rolling tired children in rugs and settling them to sleep on the sun-warmed sand...

'This'll go on for hours,' Ben said into her ear, and she felt so happy she could melt.

'Let it.'

'But you're my wife,' he said. 'Is it my fault that I want you now?'

'Yes, it is,' she said serenely. 'All your own fault. I take no responsibility.'

He grinned and held her tighter. They danced on, drowsy with love and desire, knowing they had all the time in the world for each other, but there was still this desire to have that time now.

No one looked like going home. No one wanted this party to end.

'Tell you what,' Ben said. 'Why don't we have a medical emergency?'

'An emergency?'

'A serious one,' he said. 'Did you know you can make your own phone ring?' And he twirled her over to a place where the fire torches were less bright, he whirled her round so his bride was between him and any onlookers—and, lo, his phone rang.

'Uh-huh?' he said in a voice that carried. 'Goodness, that sounds serious. Really? Well, if you say so, we'll be on our way right now.'

He replaced his phone in his jacket pocket and turned to face the bemused islanders—and his bemused and brand-new wife.

'We have an emergency on the other side of the island,' Ben said. 'It needs two doctors. Sorry, guys, keep up the party, but you need to excuse...my wife and me.'

There was a ripple of laughter and more than one mutter of disbelief.

'What sort of emergency?' someone yelled.

'Heart,' Ben said promptly. 'You can't mess with hearts.'

'Whose?' someone else yelled.

'Patient confidentiality,' Ben said. 'How can I tell you? All I can say is that it's a multiple problem. Two hearts that need attention. Ginny...Dr Koestrel can care for one, and I'll take the other.'

There was a whoop of delighted laughter. 'You're making that up,' someone else yelled. 'You just want to get away all by yourselves!'

'So what if we do?' Ben said, taking his bride by the hand and then changing his mind and sweeping her into his arms to carry her up the beach, to his waiting Jeep, to the night beyond, to the future together.

'So what if we do?' he said again. 'This is my love and my life. Have you seen my bride? If we did want to get away, all on our own, it's not our fault. It's life, guys. It's life and laughter and love and it's our future, just beyond the campfire. And, fault or not, we're stepping into it, right now.'

* * * * *

Mills & Boon® Hardback
August 2013

ROMANCE

The Billionaire's Trophy	Lynne Graham
Prince of Secrets	Lucy Monroe
A Royal Without Rules	Caitlin Crews
A Deal with Di Capua	Cathy Williams
Imprisoned by a Vow	Annie West
Duty At What Cost?	Michelle Conder
The Rings that Bind	Michelle Smart
An Inheritance of Shame	Kate Hewitt
Faking It to Making It	Ally Blake
Girl Least Likely to Marry	Amy Andrews
The Cowboy She Couldn't Forget	Patricia Thayer
A Marriage Made in Italy	Rebecca Winters
Miracle in Bellaroo Creek	Barbara Hannay
The Courage To Say Yes	Barbara Wallace
All Bets Are On	Charlotte Phillips
Last-Minute Bridesmaid	Nina Harrington
Daring to Date Dr Celebrity	Emily Forbes
Resisting the New Doc In Town	Lucy Clark

MEDICAL

Miracle on Kaimotu Island	Marion Lennox
Always the Hero	Alison Roberts
The Maverick Doctor and Miss Prim	Scarlet Wilson
About That Night...	Scarlet Wilson

Mills & Boon® Large Print
August 2013

ROMANCE

Master of her Virtue	Miranda Lee
The Cost of her Innocence	Jacqueline Baird
A Taste of the Forbidden	Carole Mortimer
Count Valieri's Prisoner	Sara Craven
The Merciless Travis Wilde	Sandra Marton
A Game with One Winner	Lynn Raye Harris
Heir to a Desert Legacy	Maisey Yates
Sparks Fly with the Billionaire	Marion Lennox
A Daddy for Her Sons	Raye Morgan
Along Came Twins...	Rebecca Winters
An Accidental Family	Ami Weaver

HISTORICAL

The Dissolute Duke	Sophia James
His Unusual Governess	Anne Herries
An Ideal Husband?	Michelle Styles
At the Highlander's Mercy	Terri Brisbin
The Rake to Redeem Her	Julia Justiss

MEDICAL

The Brooding Doc's Redemption	Kate Hardy
An Inescapable Temptation	Scarlet Wilson
Revealing The Real Dr Robinson	Dianne Drake
The Rebel and Miss Jones	Annie Claydon
The Son that Changed his Life	Jennifer Taylor
Swallowbrook's Wedding of the Year	Abigail Gordon

Mills & Boon® Hardback
September 2013

ROMANCE

Challenging Dante	Lynne Graham
Captivated by Her Innocence	Kim Lawrence
Lost to the Desert Warrior	Sarah Morgan
His Unexpected Legacy	Chantelle Shaw
Never Say No to a Caffarelli	Melanie Milburne
His Ring Is Not Enough	Maisey Yates
A Reputation to Uphold	Victoria Parker
A Whisper of Disgrace	Sharon Kendrick
If You Can't Stand the Heat...	Joss Wood
Maid of Dishonour	Heidi Rice
Bound by a Baby	Kate Hardy
In the Line of Duty	Ami Weaver
Patchwork Family in the Outback	Soraya Lane
Stranded with the Tycoon	Sophie Pembroke
The Rebound Guy	Fiona Harper
Greek for Beginners	Jackie Braun
A Child to Heal Their Hearts	Dianne Drake
Sheltered by Her Top-Notch Boss	Joanna Neil

MEDICAL

The Wife He Never Forgot	Anne Fraser
The Lone Wolf's Craving	Tina Beckett
Re-awakening His Shy Nurse	Annie Claydon
Safe in His Hands	Amy Ruttan

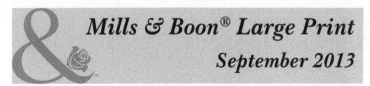

Mills & Boon® Large Print
September 2013

ROMANCE

HISTORICAL

MEDICAL

0813 GEN STD LP